I0651406

Woodruff T. Chandler

Rustic Rhymes

Woodruff T. Chandler

Rustic Rhymes

ISBN/EAN: 9783337271176

Printed in Europe, USA, Canada, Australia, Japan

Cover: Foto ©Andreas Hilbeck / pixelio.de

More available books at **www.hansebooks.com**

RUSTIC RHYMES

BY

W. T. CHANDLER, M. D.

JUDGE YE NOT MAN BY HIS FAITH,
BUT RATHER BY HIS DEEDS ;
THE PUREST MEN WHO'VE LIVED ON EARTH
ARE DAMNED BY ALL THE CREEDS.

LOUISVILLE, KY.

PRINTED FOR THE AUTHOR BY JOHN P. MORTON AND COMPANY.

1883

PREFACE.

In offering this little volume of Rustic Rhymes to the public, we are instigated by the advice of a small circle of special friends, from whom we expect nothing but the kindest reception regardless of any literary merit that may attach to the book *per se.* If, however, it should fall into the hands of strangers, we can not hope for the same leniency. Its many imperfections will necessarily call forth adverse criticisms, as perhaps none of the poems are above dull mediocrity.

The world can never excuse the unpardonable vanity of the poet presumptive, who rushes into print with the crazy infatuation that poets, like mushrooms, are born of moonlight and vapor, fed upon nothing, and reared in a single night.

The partial flattery of friends is likewise a very poor excuse for afflicting a long-suffering and much-abused public with a ragged tome of insipid doggerel; but still, you know, "a book's a book, though there's nothing in it."

As to ourself—if it be proper to speak of ourself—we make no pretense to learning. Our education has been very limited; and, though we have the doubtful certificate of a medical diploma, we boast no great proficiency in Hippocratic scholarship, and yet we have managed to eke out a precarious living at its practice. But if our youth, illiteracy, and a medical degree are not sufficient excuses for the folly of poetizing, then are we undone, and may the Lord and the critics have mercy upon our soul, for we are helpless.   W. T. CHANDLER.

CAMPBELLSVILLE, KY., April 10, 1883.

CONTENTS.

—✳—

CONTENTS.

CONTENTS.

7

RUSTIC ✽ RHYMES.

INTRODUCTION.

Each nation, grand, has its constitution
Circumventing its civic institution;
Each church its learned dogma and creed,
Wherein the orthodox are agreed.
Some ruling spirit seems to exact
Obedience from life in every act.
Its magic wand, with touch sublime,
Shapes all the destinies of time
And guides the iron wheel of fate
O'er society, o'er church and state.
As to constitution, who'll blame one,
We've had no time yet to frame one;
And should we imitate our friends,
'T would surely serve some selfish ends.

As to politics, we'll have none;
Very small's the machine we run.
We have a faith that can abide
The nation's and the people's pride;
Tho' we've seen, in our day at least,
The purest minds are most modest,
But the loud-bellowing patriots
Are wont to sop official pots.
All their glory, in the outcome,

2 (9)

Is measured by its pabulum,
The memories of our illustrious dead
Are transformed into meat and bread,
Eulogiums from pompous asses
Intended to enthuse the masses,
All demagogues' artful device,
Baiting the emoluments of office.
We'll keep ourself *in statu quo*,
And watch the winds which way they blow—
Peradventure even we may ride
To glory on some popular tide,
Yellow fever or repudiation,
Or perhaps from Buncombe station.
When fiercest factions rend the skies,
Fame nabs the unknown for compromise;
Glory reigns in caucus disorders,
Where party machines trim the borders,
And hungry asses stand and bray,
Kick, and pull for corn and hay.
Fame falls, by mere chance directed,
Like euchre on bowers, unexpected;
Who can predict official fatness
Yet in store for coming greatness?
But for ourself we'll be content,
Justice of Peace or President.

As to religion, we are emphatic,
Not of that class you call fanatic;
We think 't enough to mortals given
That all men should get to heaven.
As to a hell, 't is a disgrace
To any god, of any race,
Inspired by priestly hate and fears
To extort toll from human tears.

As to the priest, his is a trade
By which he gets his meat and bread;
The living taxed, the dead belied,
To feast his pleasure and his pride.
We scorn all theologic prating,
All schismatic hypothecating;
Ev'ry dogma and ev'ry creed
Is a hybrid of priestly breed—
A mongrel of the human race,
Fathered by superstition base.
We extend to all a cordial hand,
For God's glory or good of man.
We would not quench the hope so dear
That stays one grief or dries one tear;
We'd only chain the foul vampires
Who feast upon human desires.
Nor will we ever barb a dart
'Gainst the religion of the heart.
Sacred are all its hopes and fears,
Sacred are all its smiles and tears,
The tenderest chords that thrill the heart,
The deepest wounds, the keenest smart;
Nor would we laugh the hopes to scorn
Where immortality is born.
But, when hypocrisy dons its war-paints,
We'll ask the credentials of the saints.
If 't is not ungenerous, we shall expect
The sheets well balanced for the elect.
Where Heaven has little directed,
Surely Heaven has little expected.
The frailties of animated sod
Are measured by the mercies of God,
And not by that o'er-righteous clan
Who've less patience than God with man.

We'd teach mankind a higher truth
Than poisoning minds of tender youth;
Leaving the church's vapory brood,
Attend strictly to human good;
Leave all schisms to the priestly clan,
Ours a higher God and nobler man.

As to society, we are non-committal
On which side we intend to whittle.
There is, no doubt, some unmixed good
In patrician or plebeian blood.   .
But if life's a picture funny,
'T is an aristocrat short of money;
Too proud to beg, to work's a shame,
His stock in trade's his family name.
.   Scorning with disdainful smile
The wicked world's deceitful guile,
His great grandpa went to Congress,
Or at least was Justice o' the Peace;
Hence he boasts a title, you see,
With the honored suffix F. F. V.

Scarce less ludicrous for indictment,
Who reaps the wealth of excitement—
Perhaps 't was gold, at least 't was oil,
Found by accident on his soil;
And thus by luck, and not pursuance,
He leaps from poverty to affluence.
His rustic lass doffs linsey for silk,
And churns piano instead of milk.
The mother, o'er proud, as she ought to,
Hunts a foreign count for her daughter;
Or lavishes half of the farm
To get the family a coat of arm.

Ah! menial pride of foolish men,
One blood courses thro' every vein;
Liberty should e'er be your pride,
With equal rights to none denied.
He's the weakest vassal of earth
Who's no grandeur but titled birth—
The purple blood of royal scrub,
As thin as soapsuds in a tub;
As well had the ass delight to trace
The genealogy of his race,
Or monkey boast the creative design
That made a man without a mind.
True manhood is the gift of heaven
No father to his son has given,
Not smould'ring flames of waning fires,
Degenerate from illustrious sires;
A soul that's free, a liberal mind,
Ample by nature's own design,
Proud in truth, modest in worth,
Such the real prince of earth.
Then here it is we take our stand—
Excuse the frailties of brother man,
For frailties every man betide,
But wickedness, not frailty, is pride.
Pride, the mother of vice and crime,
Besmears the soul with filthy slime.
We'd plant virtue in every breast,
Defend mankind where'er oppressed,
Unfurl the banner of the free,
Fight tyranny and hypocrisy;
And may we die ne'er misgiving
The world is better for our living.

THE CONCLAVE OF WITCHES.

The sun went down in blackest gloom,
The night unlit by star or moon,
The angry storms darkly lowered,
The lightnings flashed and thunder roar'd,
The winds screamed like a frightened child,
The rain poured down in torrents wild;
Speedy gleams breaking through clouds
Displayed the night all draped in shrouds.
Deep in the shadow of a wood,
"Where ghost and owlets nightly brood,"
A gray old church stood on a sward,
Ev'ry approach through its graveyard;
Its crumbling roof was falling in,
Through open door rushed the wild wind;
The surging storms through ev'ry pane
In fury poured the hail and rain.
The sudden darkness streams all bright,
The church's lit with unearthly light,
The flames lick out the cracks among
As fiercely darts a serpent's tongue.
Like spectral ghosts guarding the throng,
The gravestones cast their shadows long;
A fitting place, 'mid fitting greetings,
Here the witches hold their meetings.

Long days ago, in years far passed,
Within this sacred edifice
The righteous had truth expounded,
Evil thoughts were e'en confounded.
Luckless the day, its powers strayed,
A witch, within its walls arrayed,

Condemned to death by priestly mission
And burned by holy inquisition.
From that day the powers of hell
Against the goodly mansion fell.
Old Satan did nightly roaring,
The priest himself was caught w——g!
Ev'ry sister who stepped astray
Was by nature exposed straightway;
And 't did seem with cause the least
All their temptations increased.
Ill brewed the drink the brothers drank,
Never a drop but they were drunk.
From bad to worse the day extended,
The priest was mobbed, the church suspended;
The elements given free play,
The wooden structures fell away;
The very air was foully tainted;
The rustics said " th' house was haunted."
Many a story quaint and old,
And many a scene strange and droll,
The country legends 'round afford
'Bout the old church and its graveyard—
Grand occasion of which we write.
Satan, prince of darkness and night,
Brews the winds and mad'ns the storms,
Blackens the clouds, the lightning warms;
'T is only 'mid the darkest gloom
The witch can ride upon her broom,
When wicked ghosts hover o'er graves
And demons fly from their caves—
A much-famed feast, known far and wide,
Old Nick himself was to preside;
All witches had been invited,
Famous ones were to be knighted,

The ghost of witches long departed,
Who'd died in the faith strong-hearted,
From Endor's witch, by Scripture tossed,
To every soul at Salem lost,
Demons and wizards all intent
On a blasphemous sacrament,
Where from skull-cups infernal queens
Quaff human blood and laugh like fiends.

Scarce had the day been draped in night
Or church lit up with hellish light,
Attracted by the lurid flame
On ev'ry wind the witches came;
Silently the infernal wenches
Arrayed along the broken benches,
And the devil, like one in state,
Sat where the pulpit was of late.
His fiendship first the silence broke;
From 'neath his arm he took a book
Wherein each witch, as witches should,
Had writ her name with her own blood;
And slowly, as he called the roll,
A solemn yea answered each soul.
Never a traitor could be found,
And none were missing—no, not one.
Then 'rose the chaplain o' the conclave—
A haggard wizard, thin and grave—
Raising his hands with solemn care,
"Let all the witches bow in prayer."
Then bowed each wench the humble knee,
And amen'd oft' his blasphemous plea:
"O thou great power infernal,
Who ruleth in hell eternal,
Black are thy dismal halls of night,

Woeful the victims of thy might;
Black are the trophies that we bring
To grace thy throne, infernal king.
Famine, pestilence, and dire woes
Roll their sweet savor in thy nose;
Demons, witches, and politicians
Are the engines of thy missions;
Hypocricy's thy sweetest feast
In lawyer's soul or heart o' priest,
Depraved virtue's a hallowed right
Within thy courts, O Prince of Night!
We bow before thee, willing slaves,
Thou filleth the world with woe and graves;
Bow before thee with contrite hearts,
Thou poisoneth life in all its parts;
We thank thee for this murky night,
Thank thee for each infernal right,
Thank thee for all power leased
To murder men or torture beast;
Thou art the devil, we're thy clan,
Forever and forever.   Amen!"

Then donned the priest a long black gown
With flaming demons painted 'round,
An altar quickly improvised,
Whereon he offered sacrifice,
And first his censer high he swung,
Filled with all vice and human wrong;
The curling smoke, fanned to a blaze,
Inhaled the witches until crazed;
Then in the fire the victims, paired,
By melting flames soon were charred;
Two living babes the flames indent,
Stole by a witch from a convent.

Down came the devil with his book,
A coal from off the altar took,
Touching the tongue of his own priest
Him quickly changed into a beast;
Then, with water infernally blessed,
With ceremonial charms impressed,
Formulized, and with magic said,
He sprinkled o'er each witch's head.

Then spoke the prince: "My trusted friends,
On you my earthly cause depends.
You are all mine; I claim the right
To lead you in this feast to-night,
But first, by hell's own blazing glare
You must your fealty now declare,
Renounce for e'er all hope of mercy,
Blaspheme your God, and worship me."

Then shook the hall with gleeful shout
As ev'ry witch her oath poured out;
Loud rang the night with wierd song
As ev'ry witch boasted her wrong—
How human hopes all are blasted,
The wells dried up, the fruit wasted,
How men pine with disease and pain,
Tortured by necromantic bane,
All to delight the conjurer's heart,
Perfecting her infernal art.

Then spoke the prince: "'Tis my command,
Go spread destruction o'er the land.
You have the power to break all peace;
Go torture men and torture beast,
Fill all the world with crime and woe,

Infect the rich and rob the poor,
And all whom you love shall be great,
Maimed and deformed all whom you hate."

But there was one, this very night,
First to receive the mystic rite,
Confined within the gloomy loft
And guarded by a grim, black dwarf,
Waiting the ballot to impart
Her fitness for the witch's art.

Then spoke the prince: "A sister peer
Seeks entrance to the mysteries here.
I'll pass the skull; now close inspect,
For one white ball will her reject."
He passed the skull from left to right,
And ev'ry ball was black as night.
Again he said, "With crime full due,
Well vouched she comes—the ballot's true.
Admit the wench; let ev'ry peer
Take heed on what she enters here."

All was ready for the black rite;
The hall was lit with hellish light,
The witches all in shrouds were dressed,
Skull and cross-bones on ev'ry breast;
A coffin stood within the room
Whereon was ope a magic tome—
The famous book the sybils wrote
Of magic charm and antidote,
Wherein each witch, since Noah's ark,
Had signed her name or made her mark.
With solemn pomp and eldrich brag
The dwarf ushered the wretched hag;

The witches croaked rather than sung
The initial song with wierd tongue.
But time'll fail me, if not my muse,
To tell all the mysteries they use,
Blasphemous oaths, unearthly groans,
Cups of skull, necklace of bones,
Owl-skins stuffed and poisonous toad
Winking on the unhallowed brood,
Till 't last before the witches' book,
Undaunted still by word or look,
The novice stood in triumph bold
And signed away her life and soul.
From her own arm was drawn the blood
That inked the page with crimson flood,
Then 'round her neck a serpent coiled,
And in her heart its venom boiled;
The witches gathered hand in hand
And welcomed her to witchcraft band.

There was one witch within the clan—
Most famous witch in all the land—
A blear-eyed wench, a toothless crone,
With pointed chin and hunched backbone,
Never a witch 'mong all the feast
Could freight such woe on man or beast,
Could bring such drouth or raise such storm,
Ferment more scandal or keep 't warm.
She breathed on man infected spray,
And quick he pined and died away.
When cows came home at early morn
With broken leg or missing horn,
The rustics 'round knew well the cause—
Her magic skill 'bove human laws.
They'd seen her brew her hellish arts

From serpent heads and lizard hearts;
When traveling thro' the swamps at night
They'd seen her lantern gleaming bright—
Followed, it lead through bogs and mires,
Across deep streams, through brush and briars;
How oft they'd ta'en sleeve from an arm
Or crossed themselves to break her charm;
They'd seen her in the blackest storms,
They'd seen her in a thousand forms,
Moping around dark hollow caves
Or digging bones from out old graves,
Collecting lizards, snails, and bugs,
Or poisonous herbs in broken jugs,
Changing her shape by magic wand
As oft as caprice might demand.

A lad once gave his love a rose;
In its leaflet metamorphosed
Was this old witch, and from that day
The blooming lass slow pined away.

Huntsmen, for miles around her place,
Could n'er urge their dogs to chase.
But once a hunter and his hound
Hunted a hind within this ground;
As oft he fired his bullets veered,
Tho' n'er before his aim had erred.
A silver ball crossed with a heart—
Such balls uncharm congery's art—
He straightway fired; only a groan,
A cloud of smoke, the hind was gone.
Then rushed he to the witch's den,
Broke ope her door barred from within;
There the wretched hag was found,

Bleeding from a new-made wound.
By her chimney-corner sat
A big black bug large as a cat;
A horse no larger than a mouse
Galloped fiercely around her house;
A hairy bird, a mongrel fowl,
Hybrid between the wolf and owl,
Sat grimly, the ashes among,
Eating fire with serpent tongue;
Frogs, spiders, and snakes unnumbered
'Round her wretched hovel slumbered.
He raised his hand to strike the fiend,
But darkness held its vail between.
As if on an enchanted spray,
He felt himself borne far away;
And next he found himself in bed,
Full daylight streaming overhead;
The cunning witch would have it seem
He'd only wounded her in dream.

This witch was to receive the order,
Knighthood's most famous star and garter,
Many a coward and many a flirt
Have worn its insignia with less desert.
First bowed the witch in low station,
Like a queen for coronation;
Then stepped old Satan softly down,
His magic wand by serpents wound,
And waving 'bove the kneeling wight
He bade her, "Arise, Madam Knight;"
Then broke silence with fearful yell,
As encored the imps of hell,
And flopping around the house blazed
Until the witches fairly crazed.

And now the banquet table's spread
Where all must feast from human dead,
And cups of skull and knives of bone
Are freely 'round the table strewn,
And only blood, but not of beast,
Is consecrated for the feast.
Old Nick presides with heart content,
And passes 'round the sacrament.
When all were served he raised a skull
With briny gore still dripping full,
And ere he drank offered a toast
To all the witches and the ghost;
Then to his lips he pressed the cup
And drank till ev'ry drop dried up;
Ordered the tables cleared at once
And ev'ry witch out to the dance;
As for music to warm their legs
And stir the witches on their pegs,
An orchestra from Fiddler's Green
Imported special for this scene;
A hundred fiddlers cross'd their bows,
A hundred witches quickly rose;
And to and fro the wenches prance,
The Devil leading in the dance.
And as the stormy night wore on
The dancers kept their pace till morn,
Till rising sun with silver ray
Rolled back the dusky clouds from day;
With the gray streaks that pierced the gloom
Each weary witch got on her broom
And winged her flight on the first spray
That fled before advancing day.

THE THREE FUNERALS.

At early morn December winds
  Blew fierce o'er ice and snow,
As 'long a pompous funeral train
  Moved solemnly and slow;
Silver casket and hearse of glass,
  Drawn by steed nobly bred,
A hundred coaches filed behind
  In honor of the dead.

They laid him 'neath a marble shaft
  Sculptured in lordly pride;
As o'er him heaped winter flowers
  Never an eye was dried.
The great of earth were gathered there,
  The nation heard the groans,
Marching around his resting-place,
  Paid honor to his bones.

Music and tears for the funeral hir'd,
  Grief the few only felt;
They laid him 'way in a costly vault,
  And left him there to melt.
Even the man of God was there,
  All dressed in priestly gown,
He spoke a requiem for th' dead,
  And called it sacred ground.

'T is noon, but still the bitter winds
  Are driven o'er the plain,
The drifting clouds still veil the sun
  Anon with snow and rain.

Another scene, but oh, how changed!
   Toward the pauper's field
A rude coffin in a ruder cart,
   And loudly screeches each wheel.

Where now 's the pompous funeral train
   In honor of the dead?
A weeping widow sits alone
   Upon the coffin's lid.
Where now 's the soft and solemn tones
   Lent by music's sad charms?
Only the half-clad orphan's wail
   Within the mother's arms.

Where now 's the steed of noble sires
   Which with black plumelets wave?
Only the stubborn oxen tread
   Sullenly to the grave.
O, where 's the sacred man of God
   Who soothes the widow's fears?
Sent by a kindest Providence
   To dry the orphan's tears.

Not there! not there! the howling priests
   Hear but the sound of gold;
You 'll find them at the rich man's grave
   Cheering the drooping soul.
The poor must plod life's downward way,
   Unremembered their tears;
The rich man feasts the preacher's ease
   And must enjoy his prayers.

As the clods fall low on the coffin
   The hollow echoes start,

The ruthless winds sweep madly by,
  Cold as the human heart.
The widow weeps, the orphans cry,
  The sexton plies his spade,
And all 'lone by the friendless grave
  Their last sad rights are paid.

Eve's slanting sun thro' broken clouds
  By fitful beams was stealing,
For nature ofttimes has a smile
  Where man has no feeling.
Another funeral-scene behold,
  Now from the almshouse goes
A box that might for coffin serve
  Or to hold potatoes.

The gleeful driver cracks his whip,
  His old horse strikes a trot,
And 'long the busy street they rush—
  The throng regard them not.
On they go to the potter's field,
  No knells with solemn toll,
The merry sexton blithely sings
  While filling up the hole.

But why lament the pauper's fate?
  Unconscious still he lies,
Nor feels the jolts nor hears the jests
  Nor cares for earth's memories.
No widow weeps with broken heart,
  No orphans swell her groans;
The voice of pride 's an empty show—
  God 'll take care of his bones.

The rich sleep in their marble vaults,
   And costly mass is said;
The pauper rests in the potter's field,
   Where never a tear's shed.
The prayers of church, the praise of wealth,
   Will 'wake Dives no more,
Nor the smile of pity, contempt, or scorn
   Ever disturb the poor.

THE CALL.

Where blooms the classic pennyroyal
   Upon the red-knolled hills,
And shin-briars in serpent coil
   Add to the plowman's ills,
When August shoots its boiling rays
   From out a copper sky,
And all the fields are in a blaze,
   The cooling streams are dry,

A weary lad, with dust and sweat
   Covered from toes to crown,
With blistered face and torn feet,
   Slowly plowed the field 'round;
His stubborn mule balked with mule pride
   Till all his temper burst,
Plow-handles gored him in the side
   Until he cried and cursed.

'Tis dinner time: at sultry noon,
   Stretched by a stagnant stream,

And half awake and half in swoon,
    Strange visions fill his dream ;
From out the wood it was he heard,
    Perhaps the owlet's screech,
Or voice of heaven's sovereign Lord,
    "'Rise, young man, and go preach."

Full soon the theocratic school
    To his pious soul appealed ;
He quit shin-briars, plow, and mule
    To till the cleric field ;
A black cloth coat and fine silk hat,
    For plowman's humble fare—
Chicken well fried for bacon fat,
    And town grease for his hair.

Mule and plowman yield to the call,
    Off to conference straight.
And next we hear them bray and bawl
    On a mountain circuit.
Full oft he tells by love-feast rule
    About that sultry day
When from shin-briars, plow, and mule
    The Lord called him away.

We 've heard him tell this artless tale,
    Served like a confection,
With smiles and tears and horrid wail
    Exhorting a collection ;
And, as the mission box went 'round
    Where the elect were bowing,
We 've thought we heard the nickels sound—
    'T is better far than plowing.

THE ALAMO.

So long as deeds of chivalry
   Their kindling flames impart,
The heroes of the Alamo
   Will fire the patriot's heart;
They fell indeed like heroes
   With lives to country given,
Their feet toward the foe,
   Their faces to the heaven.

This noble band of Texans
   Will keep her fame alive,
With Thermopyla's Leonidas
   The Alamo braves survive;
Engraved on Freedom's banner,
   Unfurl it to the gale;
Their swords drawn for Liberty,
   Their lives in the scale.

Oh! ye who as softly die
   As twilight dews are spread,
Gaze upon the bloody wall,
   The Alamo and its dead;
Can ye look upon the carnage—
   Look with a tearless eye
Where Crockett and Bowie fell,
   And were but proud to die?

Look at Alamo's bloody field,
   Texas' immortal band descry,
Heaping a bed of Mexicans
   On whom to fall and die;

Dying indeed as brave men,
  Crimson with Freedom's gore,
The heroes of Texan liberty,
  Eternal as th' Alamo.

Together they stood, together fell;
  No shrink from death's grim jaws
Where the earth with sacred blood
  Was stained in Freedom's cause;
Ev'ry man died at his gun,
  Braved till death each fiery blast;
But Alamo fell only there
  When had fallen the last.

Still around the Mexican States,
  More terrible than a living foe,
Hover in their ghostly forms
  The specters of the Alamo;
They were at Buena Vista,
  Cheering Taylor's immortal braves,
And when the bugle sounds again
  Will rise from out their graves.

No marble shaft needs to tell
  Posterity their story,
Carved on fame's eternal scroll
  Are their names of glory;
They will live with patriots true,
  Embalmed in Freedom's breast,
So long as America's great
  Will share its greatness.

The spectral ghost of grizzly death
  The cowardly heart o'erawes,

But they are wrapped in glory's shroud
  Who die in Freedom's cause.
The tears of a grateful country
  Flow for its martyred free—
Bravest men, who thus nobly die
  For home and liberty.

NATURE'S GOD.

Who can not see God in the light
  On land or ocean wide,
Where fierce tornadoes speak his might
  And dark storms swell his pride,
Or yet serene in gentle twilight,
  As fades the day in coolly hours,
The stars that deck the canopied night,
  The glory of the flowers?

Ask not revelation for its proof;
  Let the soul itself inspire;
Read from nature's book of truth,
  Engraved in ev'ry desire.
Trace we not, through ages past,
  Nature's calms and nature's shocks,
God's tender mercy and his awful wrath
  Written on the ancient rocks?

Through misty depths of ether afar
  Behold the grandeur of his might,
His name inscribed on ev'ry star,
  Traced with worlds in circling flight.

Who has not seen the lightning's flash
   Like daylight thro' broken cloud?
Who has not heard the thunder's crash,
   As 'fore the winds th' forest bow'd?

Is God not in the ocean wild,
   In lovely flowers' modest form,
As gentle as a tender child,
   As fierce as the thunder-storm?
Oh, let us learn, without the shame
   Superstitions alone endure,
God has written his eternal name,
   And his name is—Nature.

THE PROTRACTED MEETING.

We've had a big meeting of late,
   Stirred pious and uncivil;
Some have seen the pearly gate,
   And some have seen the devil.
Saintly shouting was appended,
   Of the Lord's own selection,
And the meeting fitly ended
   With a great big collection.

The preacher told an awful tale
   About one fiery lake,
Where burning souls did naught but wail
   Before a monster snake.
The women screamed and wept by fits,
   Frightened at his diction,

Till all the children lost their wits—
  This he called conviction.

The priest whined a dolorous strain,
  Pounded the sacred book,
Till windows rattled ev'ry pane,
  And roof and rafters shook.
Then, howling like the midnight storms
  Groaning through hollow caves,
Grouped the dead in frantic forms
  Around their shrunken graves.

Through lurid flames a monster shone,
  Grim, savage, and cruel,
Seated with flesh-fork on his throne,
  Roasting souls for fuel.
And now commenced a great stampede
  Toward the mourner's-bench,
Where little children took the lead,
  And followed man and wench.

With nasal twang the choir sang
  A chorus to the crying,
And every song was drawled out long,
  To imitate the dying.
The Spirit fell from out the sky,
  Just like a water-spout,
As oft was heard the natal cry
  With loud resounding shout.

With awful yells they charged on sin,
  Beyond all pencil-painting;
The fearful shrieks maddened the din—
  Souls half crazed, half fainting.

4

Some gnash and foam, wildly convulsed;
　Some like demons dance;
Some fall as dead, with hearts unpulsed,
　And dream in holy trance.

Until at length the preachers speak:
　"'Tis late; we must have rest;
The spirit's willing, the flesh is weak,
　However much we're blessed.
We'll meet again to-morrow night,
　Without divine restriction;　　*
The evidence of grace is bright;
　Receive the benediction."

1880—1881.

The old year is dying—let it die
　With all the joys and cares,
And on the tombstone of the past
　Be engraved with other years.
Why should we remember it now,
　When, like a fading dream,
We must trust a treacherous memory
　For all that it has been?

But there are hours in its memory
　Seared deeply in the heart,
Hours that taught living lessons
　From which we ne'er can part;
Let us strew them all with flowers,
　Where kindest thoughts attend,

As we would deck the quiet grave
Of best and dearest friend.

Oh! where are those we used to love,
Who 've passed with the year and gone;
Will they come no more to see us
When all is quiet at home?
When we muse in our solitude
In the fancies of our dream,
Their faces will pass before us
In shadowy pantomime.

And as the shades of other years
Are falling quickly 'round us,
Memory traces back the days
When boyhood's fancies bound us;
Many a bright and radiant hope,
Mingled with bitterest cares,
Is left engraved upon the heart
In memory of other years.

The past, like its forgotten dead
Who were once its living slaves,
Is only now to be revealed
By the marks upon its graves;
And the darkness gathering round it
In the distance grows profound;
The mountains tossed, the valleys torn,
Are but the scars of its wound.

Then let the old year die in peace—
Shed no sorrowing tears o'er it,
It will soon be lost in the past,
With millions gone before it.

In other years when other men,
　In turning nature's page,
Look back upon our ancient time
　And wonder on our age;

When the learn'd Archæologist,
　In delving 'mong our sods,
Speculates on our sciences
　And fables out our gods;
When broken arch and fallen shaft
　Are crumbling in decay
O'er the graves of mighty nations
　Long since passed away.

ENGLAND.

England, our mother country,
　Still struggling to be free,
Thou art lashed with iron chains
　To the ghost of royalty;
Look out from thy sea-washed home
　Across the swelling deep,
Behold the ensign of the free,
　And hang thy harp and weep.

The dog that serves his master
　May share his master's fate,
The slaves that wait on royalty
　May sup from golden plate;
Far better, like the hungry wolf,
　To roam the forest free—

The scanty crums of honest toil
　Are sweetened with liberty.

Slaves to proud aristocracy—
　Poor fawning menial things—
Thy very bards are forced to sing
　The praises of thy kings;
Thy church, like thy royal state,
　Is of regal pedigree,
Its highest meed to man or God
　Is kingly sovereignty.

Oh! where is thy ancient valor?
　Where do thy heroes dwell?
Can Liberty awake no more
　The spirit of a Cromwell?
Are slavery's chains so pleasant
　Ye wear its iron bands?
Is the regal blood divine,
　Ye lick its crime-stained hands?

Do ye think your monarchs true?
　Think ye they hear your groans?
They 'd brain your very children
　Between them and their thrones.
Why should ye, whom God has made
　With blood as pure and free,
Be mere serfs to bloated kings,
　Slaves to sovereignty?

Down with your kings, down with your priest—
　Lords of ev'ry degree—
Who rob the toiling millions
　For their own luxury.

When the nations are enlightened,
　Farewell these pampered knaves;
When superstition 's buried,
　They 're buried in its graves.

Awake, ye son of Slavery,
　Awake, ye slumb'ring band!
Assert the rights of equality
　God gives to ev'ry man.
Pattern after the glory
　The land that calls thee mother;
Teach thy kings some useful trade,
　And thy priest some other.

THE GRAVEYARD.

In pensive mood I sit me down
　In this city of the dead,
And muse upon the world around.
Mortal men, by destiny bound,
One by.one approach this ground
　In mournful funeral tread.

I see the living come and go
　In search of joy and treasure,
Thoughtless of those who here lie low,
With spreading trees high towering o'er,
Who 'll 'wake from their sleep no more
　Till God speaks his pleasure.

Once they thronged the marts of life
　With busy hopes and cares;
And what of joy and what of strife
As father, mother, husband, or wife,
'Mid Time's fleeting scenes was rife,
　Had their smiles and tears!

Here they lie in moldering waste,
　In stinking carnage rotten,
And hither all the human race,
All driven by destiny, haste
Where sleep the teeming millions past—
　By all but God forgotten.

I mark the graves of many dead,
　Some blooming with flowers,
And sweetest fragrance o'er them shed,
Where living friends, by kindness led,
Still linger around this last bed
　To cheer its lonely hours.

Some amid weeds and briars sleep,
　Hid 'way from mortal sight;
They had few friends who cared to weep,
None their memories sought to keep;
But God 'll watch each moldering heap
　Through Time's long dark night.

I read, engraved on marble shaft,
　Words o' trembling hopes and fears;
I knew some faces ere they left
(May God their souls heavenward waft),
I saw their friends, in tears, bereft,
　Filled with sorrowing cares.

On each white stone's a name and age,
    With panegyrics o' worth ;
I mark that death in fiery rage
Spared neither babe, rustic, or sage ;
And wealth or rank had no prestige
    Nor privilege of birth.

But oh ! to see where Faith, dying,
    Carves in stone cold as death
Fond hopes that take no denying ;
On wings of peace the soul, flying,
Leaves the world without sighing,
    Nor dreads the grave beneath :

" Gone home," " Sweetest sleep," " Fondest rest,"
    Epitaphs that greet the eye,
As if the grave as lightly pressed
As downy couch on weary breast,
And sweetest dreams but manifest
    How pleasant 't is to die.

And some have here been sleeping
    Since long before my day ;
But for epitaphs, in keeping
With sorrowing mortals weeping,
I'd never know these mounds heaping
    Held aught of human clay.

Ah ! sad to think, some future time,
    As its circling flight extends,
O'er my grave, some friend of rhyme,
Led by chance to death-cold shrine,
May read upon a slab of mine
    The last farewell of friends.

ADVICE TO A YOUNG FRIEND.

Young man, though the world seems fair
    When abroad.you wander,
Place your feet with modest care
    Lest they slip from under.
Pleasure and its allurements bright,
    With passion's wild desire,
Is like an ignis-fatuus light
    Leading through the mire.

Ev'ry where the snares of death
    Are thickly set around you,
Gory vice with mephitic breath
    Poisons life to wound you.
The wiles o' wealth, the smiles o' woman,
    Conspire to deceive you;
Ev'ry heart that beats is human,
    And sorely may grieve you.

The gaudy show of glittering wealth
    Will tempt you to its shame;
Of little worth is wordly pelf,
    Foul with dishonor's stain;
Far better poor, the humble part
    Nature's wealth has given;
The treasures of an honest heart
    Bear exchange in heaven.

Beware of passion's foul delight,
    Let virtue reign supreme;
E'en Satan was an angel bright
    Before he was a fiend;

The siren voice of wicked beauty
    Enslaves you with its spell
Till conscience, estranged from duty,
    Leaves the soul in hell.

Beware of wine, the sparkling cup,
    Oh ne'er become its slave!
Tho' beauty's hand should fill it up,
    'T is manhood's darkest grave;
Hidden serpents in deadly toil
    Lurk beneath its venom cold,
Fast 'round your heart they will coil
    And breathe their virus in your soul.

Beware the aristocratic brood
    Who make labor a disgrace,
Pride themselves on family blood
    Or ancient titled race;
With heart and hand, nerve and brain,
    Meet life's contending broils—
If you'd reap the harvest gain,
    You must share the summer toils.

Beware the world's changing faces,
    Scan the motives of each breast;
The merry face is social graces,
    The sober one is business.
Beware, unless you mistake them
    With their thousand cunning guiles,
As you meet you'll have to take them
    Whether fortune frowns or smiles.

Politicians are wont to awe you
    With liberty's certain knell,

Priest and prophets too would draw you,
  Frightened by a blazin' hell ;
But politics was made for fools,
  To officer the lazy,
And religion in all its schools
  Will surely run you crazy.

Beware, then, fanatic preachers
  Of ev'ry faith and creed,
The rant of schismatic teachers
  In counsel never heed ;
God surely is not so gory
  Some to damn, some to elect,
Yet nature's God in nature's glory
  Ev'ry creature should respect.

THE CHILD'S PRAYER.

When softly the night came down
  O'er fields and forest gray,
A little child at evening tide
  Kneeled alone to pray ;
And on the golden sunset rays,
  By lingering twilight given,
The angels bore her simple prayer
  Up to the gates of heaven.

In simple and confiding tones
  It bubbled from her breast :
" Now I lay me down to sleep—
  God knows all the rest."

I 've heard prayer, in temples grand,
    Chanted to empty space,
But never prayer so pure, so sweet,
    Filled with heavenly grace.

I 've heard prayer, all written out
    To suit the times and hours,
That flowed gently as summer streams
    Rippling o'er beds of flowers;
But all vain mockery to measure
    Proud human glory by,
To please the dull ear of mortals,
    Never to reach the sky.

How sweet and simple, yet sublime,
    No human thoughts compare,
Words gathered from a mother's lips,
    And lisped again in prayer;
No wonder that the Master said,
    Ye all have vainly striven,
Lest ye become as little children
    Ye can not enter heaven.

Oh! for that faith, that child-like trust,
    That binds one to the skies,
Stronger than the powers of death
    To sever human ties;
That faith that loves and never doubts,
    Howe'er the skeptic pleads,
But trusts heaven's generous care
    For all its human needs.

Would that I were a child to-night,
    Bowing by mother's knee,

Lisping again the simple prayers
  Her tender love taught me ;
But I've grown old in sin and doubt,
  My conscience pleads in vain—
Would that I could forget it all
  And be a child again.

THE SONG OF THE WATERS.

Come list to the songs of the waters,
  Come list to the tales they tell,
From the gentlest rain that patters,
  To the mighty ocean's swell :
"I'm a mist from off the ocean,
  I'm a cloud from off the sea,
With the wild winds in commotion
  I'm driven over the lea.

"I fall on the valleys and hills
  Where the parched earth is dry,
Seek thro' the soil and 'long the rills,
  Wand'ring the meadows by ;
The flowers bloom on verdant banks
  And smile at my coming,
Little birds with joyous pranks
  Keep time with sweet humming.

"All nature smiling greets me,
  I raise each drooping head,
On every herb that meets me,
  A thousand blessings shed ;

I pour my streams from hill-side,
    I dash the valleys through,
And on to join the mighty tide,
    Swelling its floods anew.

"Sometimes when o'er the angry deep
    The mighty storm king rides,
My surging billows furious sweep
    And lash its mountain sides;
I break the chains forged by man,
    I tear his barks in twain,
Scatter them with the ocean sand,
    Or dash them 'long the main.

"Many fair-haired sons and daughters,
    And many of earth's braves,
Gone down in my turbid waters,
    Are sleeping in my caves;
I've kissed the brow of fairest maid,
    I've lulled the bride to sleep;
'Mid coral rocks their bones are laid,
    Embalmed beneath my deep.

"From ocean beds I rise, and sail
    O'er land a misty breeze,
I fall as rain, as dew, or hail
    Upon the grass and trees;
I gladden the hearts of men and beast,
    I cool the fevered air,
I bring to thirsty earth a feast,
    The harvest follows fair.

"Now, young man, you've heard my song,
    You've heard my tale of strife,

A thousand joys for ev'ry wrong
  Sparkle my cup of life;
Come bow yourself before my shrine,
  Come sleep upon my brink,
Come swear by the will, only thine,
  Naught but water to drink."

THE NORTH AMERICAN INDIAN.

From the grave of a buried past
We view ancient nations in waste,
Mark each crumbling city and tower,
The silent records of Time's power;
From the rocks and craggy ledges
We trace the foot-prints of ages;
We see the life of ancient plains
Buried in rock, fossil remains,
Or in dried mummies from the tombs,
From Thebes' and Memphis' catacombs,
Read the history of ancient race
On hieroglyphic'd resting place.

So, America, in thy hills and glen
Is buried an ancient race of men,
Whose shadowy forms and dusky shrouds
Hang 'round thee in vapory clouds,
Haunting thy caverns, cliffs, and streams,
Like specters grim in frightful dreams.

Where agriculture plows the field,
Where commerce rolls its busy wheel,

Where villas, towns, and cities grand
Spread life and vigor o'er the land,
Here once in solitary haunts,
The forest supplying his wants,
With feud and chase and simple toil,
Lived th' aborigine of the soil;
Child of nature, artless and wild,
'Mid mountain rocks and craggy defile,
Here he was wont to make his home
And shelter from the raging storm;
Among wild beast and wilder wood,
By cataract and surging flood,
Thro' jungles deep and dark as night—
Scarce sun or moon or star could light—
Where silence rears its awful brood,
He sought his shelter and his food.

Far from luxury's sick'ning bane,
Where wealth and vice in funeral train
Lead the pomp of regal treasure,
Nauseate the soul with pleasure,
Drag man to passion's evil strife,
Enthused with artificial life,
The red man on his couch of leaves,
Vaulted heav'n his palace eves,
The dog, the bow, and rude rock knife,
His companions and friends of life.

No nobler story would he indite,
Around his wigwam-fire at night,
When inspiring the younger braves
With rev'rence for their fathers' graves,
To emulate their deeds of pride,
Famous legends in ev'ry tribe;

They told of wildest scenes in life,
Battle's array and bloody strife,
How thro' jungles dark and gory
Chieftain led the braves to glory,
Vindicated right with bravery,
Saved the tribe from menial slavery.

They told of a night, dark and damp,
A hungry wolf prowled into camp,
Forced by famine from out the wild,
To feed on man, woman, or child,
Maddened with hunger long delayed,
No more by human eye dismayed,
But scorning danger and its wrath,
Attacked a warrior in his path;
While victory faltered o'er the strife
The warrior unsheathed his flint knife,
But ere comrades drag them apart
The flint's lodged in the wolf's heart.

How an eagle, from its rocky nest,
Soared down from the mountain crest
And bore away a chieftain's boy,
Pride of the tribe, his father's joy;
Then was grief and bitter tears
Such as had not been seen for years;
Swift a young warrior in his pride
Climbed the rugged mountain side,
O'er caverns, rocks, and shaggy cliffs,
Where fleecy cloud in shadow drifts
O'er dark defile and precipitous height,
Follows the eagle in its flight,
And drives it from its mountain nest—
Returns, the boy upon his breast.

5

From these scenes of wild relation
Turn to a solemn transformation :
The forest has been swept away,
The wigwams molder in decay,
The ancient hunting-ground bereft,
And not a living Indian left
To guard his ancestral graves
Or sing the glory of the braves.

Why so swift the hand of decay,
Why has this nation passed away ?
When the mailed arm of might
Alone is arbiter of the right,
The weak can dare only to die,
And this must answer for the why.
They fell as brave men well might fall,
Fighting for country and for all,
Despising peace that would debase,
Dishonor, defile, and disgrace.

Who blames them if, in their despair,
They arose from the midnight lair,
Made villages o'er hills and dells
Hideous with their slogan yells,
Following with tomahawk and fire,
The fury of revengeful ire,
To stay the march of a nation
Whose presence was extermination ?

Who blames them if from ambuscade
The weary traveler was delayed,
Eased by the bloody scalping-knife,
Awoke no more to scenes of strife.

Who blames them, when all around
Was Heard the ax, sound on sound,
Felling the forest broad and wide,
Their happy hunting-ground, their pride,
The home of illustrious braves
Made sacred by their fathers' graves,
If they fought for rights there denied,
The defense of home and fireside?
And if too weak to stand the flood,
They sold as best they could for blood.

Where now's this ill-fated nation,
Doomed by Christian expatriation,
Chased through forest and dark defile
And hunted down like varmints wild?
A few still in the rocky west
Hang around the mountain crest,
Where now to limbs agile and fleet
The ocean impedes farther retreat;
For state on state in rapid stride
Presses them to the surging tide,
Crowded by a jealous nation,
Surely doomed to extermination.

A few more years shall roll before
These hardy sons are no more,
Their forest homes and rude war-songs
Live only in legends of wrongs;
Save now and then the scientist comes
To mar the resting of their bones,
When perchance in some grassy mound
Their implements of war are found
When searching among nature's waste
For relics of the forgotten past.

Liberty with unblushing face
Presides o'er this murdered race,
Boasting sovereign powers to defend
Ev'ry right held sacred by men.
Liberty, liberty, bright thy fame
When in name and action the same—
Not republics in federal might
To trample on the weaker right—
Thou shouldst preside where justice's done;
A million tyrants are worse than one.

THE FALLEN ANGEL.

And now she's dead upon the street,
   Clasped in winter's cold embrace,
Her form covered with icy sleet,
   The tears frozen on her face.

Do you shudder as you pass her
   With a cold and scornful frown?
Call society to disgrace her—
   She's a woman of the town.

Is there never a heart that's human,
   That can wake a kindred thrill?
Are there no pure and true men
   Who contend for mercy still?

In life's wicked variorum
   Dwells the moral law sublime,
And they are friends of decorum
   Who succeed in hiding crime.

Many a proud and vaunting beauty
  Passes by with scornful jeers ;
Should dark secrets tell all they 're true to,
  She 'd bow by this corpse in tears.

Many a pharisee, whose blame
  Looks mockingly on this scene,
Has smiled on her in dens of shame
  When night held its vail between.

So cold 's man's heart, and cold 's the world,
  Where hopeless wretches shiver,
And pride and vice in maddening whirl
  Roll darkly on forever.

THE FEVER DREAM.

I dreamed a dream, a strange, wild dream,
  Of famine and disease,
The fires flashed along the ground
  And flamed from burning trees,
Where men, frenzied with dire thirst,
  All waited their slaughter,
Grouping around in mournful groups,
  And crying for water.

I saw the beast and birds, like man,
  Parching 'neath burning sun,
Moping around a stagnant pool,
  And dying one by one ;

And where they died their stinking forms
    Bred pestilence and woe;
The living gazed on the carnage,
    But shrank from it no more,

With lips all parched and eyes blood-shot
    And bodies crisped with pains,
With stagnant blood and feverish
    Clotted in shrunken veins;
I saw the strong man slay the weak
    And drink his blood in ire,
The salty gore maddened his brain
    Kindling his thirst to fire;

I saw the mother take her babe,
    In a fit of despair,
Dash out its brain against the wall
    And end its suffering there;
Then, gazing wildly on her crime,
    Smiling in fiendish pride,
Drive a dagger to her own heart
    And sink down by its side.

Some died convulsed, some laughing died,
    The powers of hell spurning,
Such laughs as only demons laugh
    Wrapt in infernal burning;
Some lingered long in wretchedness
    Ere the finale was o'er,
Some dared to still live on and on
    Reserved for future woe.

The wicked prayed, the righteous cursed,
    For all were wont to die,

Some tried to take their own lives,
  Which nature could deny.
As I gazed the sun drew nearer,
  Its flames still hotter roll,
Till all the air seemed on fire,
  Scorching my parched soul.

I saw a grove of luscious fruit
  Ripening 'mid scenery rare,
I approached, the phantom mirage
  Dissolved in burning air;
I heard the sweet sound of waters
  Falling 'mid bowers green,
As I approached the burning air
  Spread flames throughout the scene.

I wandered long o'er torrid plains,
  O'er burning fields and dry,
Till last a grove and sparkling fount
  My fancy did espy;
As I approached the crystal stream
  To cool my burning brain,
A demon issued from his cave
  And drove me back again.

At last, o'ercome with heat and pain,
  I laid me down to die,
My bed upon the burning sand
  Beneath a burning sky;
Around me stood, in gaunt array,
  Grim specters of death,
Like famished wolves they seemed to wait
  But for my parting breath.

I saw the clouds now gathering dark
  Upon the blazing sky,
I heard the groanings of the storm,
  The thunders in reply;
I saw the drenching rain pour down
  When in the flames I turned,
But not a drop fell on my couch—
  In agony I burned.

I awoke; it was a Fever Dream
  That broke my weary sleep,
Through my own veins rolled the fire
  That parched my life so deep;
My brain was hot, my tongue was dry,
  My soul in frenzy blind,
And visions fierce and demons dire
  Stalked through my fevered mind.

IMMORTALITY.

Born of hope and born of fear,
  In the darkness stooping,
We linger 'round death's shadowy sphere
  With souls and hearts still drooping,
Out into the shadowy vagueness
  Group the wanderings of the mind,
Call on hope to light the drear'ness,
  Call on faith to sight the blind;
Then the soul from out its darkness
  Looks above the shadowed dead,
Trusts the hope that's born within it,
  Trusts to hope, and's not afraid.

Who are they with souls of vagueness,
  Who are they with hearts unblessed?
Ever groping in the darkness,
  Ever groping without rest;
If they find not God in nature,
  And their minds are tempest tossed,
If they know no creeds nor churches,
  Are their souls forever lost?
Is there not a power o'erspreading,
  Kinder than the creeds of man,
A power that shapes all life's actions
  Nor wrecks a soul upon its strand?

If perchance an erring brother
  In the darkness should mistake,
Will there from the clouds eternal
  Ne'er a ray of mercy break?
Will the soul, dark and benighted,
  Dwell forever in its night?
Will the gloom remain unlighted,
  When that soul pleads for light?
Has heaven forever sided
  With the faith that's born of fear?
Is reason fore'er derided?
  Is credulity so dear?

THE OLD MOONSHINE STILL.

In a lone dusky glen,
From the busy haunts of men
   Far in the forest away,
Where the wolf and the bear
In their dark coverts lair
   And jealously guard the day,

Where the pale moon's light,
O'er the steep craggy height,
   Peeps in the valley between,
And the shadows of the wood,
Like ghostly specters, brood
   O'er the dark, wild scene,

Where the cool, clear fountain
Dashes down the mountain,
   Only wild foot-prints intrude,
'Neath the dark shadowy hill
Is the old moonshine still,
   Steaming 'way in solitude.

From their lone, dusky caves,
Like ghouls from their graves
   Treading softly and slow,
A tortuous path wends
The wild, smutty denizens
   To the deep valley below.

Like the twilight's soft dews
That gentle evening hues
   From silver clouds distill,

As noiseless is their tread
As the homes of the dead
   In the shadows 'neath the hill.

And the moon with soft light
Looks down from the night,
   Sporting in the sparkling rill
As if 't was wont to sup,
From the old tin cup,
   A draught fresh from the still.

THE DYING DAY.

Oh! how sweet at evening tide,
   When the setting sun is low
And the lingering shadows glide
   Softly 'round the cottage door,
When the twilight many hued
   Paints the west in gold and gray,
The heart with sacred thoughts imbued
   Muses on the dying day.

Unlike the chamber of death,
   Where griefs and sorrows abound,
Where friends with abated breath
   Tread mournfully around;
But like the gentler repose,
   Where await the sweetest dreams
On downy couches to disclose
   Life's fondest, softest gleams.

As zephyrs softly lulled to sleep,
    As fades the memory of dreams
O'er life's ever turbulent deep,
    So wane the sinking beams;
Darkness steals o'er this sphere
    Like shadows o'er the soul
Weighed down with sorrowing care
    At life's wearisome goal.

Oh! may we, with soul and heart
    Moved by love in life's sad way,
From the scenes of time depart
    Serene as the dying day;
And backward o'er life's scenes
    Many happy memories trace,
As pure as the twilight's beams
    Its even paths of peace.

When life's waning sun shall fade
    In the dark gloom of night,
Oh! may no dusky clouds shade
    The glory of evening's twilight,
But softly o'er the dying sight,
    Cheered by faith and love,
May hope stream a beacon light
    From its source above.

DREAMLAND.

There is a land, a Dreamland,
  A misty and vapory sphere,
The sunshine and the shadows
  Are all its joy and care,
And the sunshine and the shadows
  As gently pass along
As floats a fleecy cloud,
  As dies a mellow song.

These fancies quaint and curious
  Are woven into form,
Long-fading recollections
  Spring into being warm,
A thousand grotesque figures
  Contend in busy strife,
Vapory forms of nothingness
  Stalk in real life.

Life itself is but a dream,
  Thro' weary hours repeating
Joys and cares, sunshine and shadows,
  Vapory and fleeting;
We gaze upon enchanted scenes,
  List' to enchanted song,
Thro' the realms of nothingness
  A dreamy existence prolong.

Hie me away to this fairy land,
  Where beauties resplendent beam,
Let the shadowy cares of life
  Pass in a fleeting dream;

Oh let me drown the grim woes
   To real existence given,
If 't is only fancy's repose,
   Let me dream 't is heaven.

DEPARTED YOUTH.

It fills my heart with a solemn thrill
   To think of days now gone,
When in boyish pride I climbed the hill—
And my youthful fancy wanders still,
   Plucking each rose and thorn.

Scenes of my youth dear to my heart,
   Tho' saddest memories trace,
And many a joy and many a smart
From out the past like shadows start
   And meet me face to face.

In the gloom of the faded past,
   Like the meteor's sudden light,
Bright gleams start from out its waste
Of days and months and years past
   To oblivion's dark blight.

I gaze on youth with abated breath,
   I count its days again,
Each fading hour a scene of death,
Each dying day millions bereft
   In sorrow and in pain.

The past is but a world of graves
  Where untold millions lie,
And echoing thro' its dusky caves
Eternity's murky stream laves
  With muffled minstrelsy.

Where'er I wander, my feet still tread
  On the graves of those I knew,
From each shadow.faces of the dead
Meet me with years that long have fled,
  Their friendship to renew.

Thro' all these scenes one joyous truth
  Relieves my heart from pain,
I'll rejoin the friends of my youth,
Nor the scythe of Time with pitiless ruth
  Shall sever us again.

BLUSHES.

In the vivid blushes
  That mantle the cheek
The red blood rushes ·
  Its language to speak,
Our passions disclosing,
  Our thoughts revealing,
As plainly exposing
  Each secret feeling.

There's a blush for love,
  Still another for shame,

They seem to move
　Like a kindling flame;
Love has gentle hues,
　Like the fading twilight,
Ere the darkness imbues
　The dusky night;

But disgrace and shame
　Are of the deepest dye,
As the lightning's flame
　On a stormy sky.
Each different expression,
　So strangely wrought,
Is the silent confession
　Of a secret thought.

The blush of modesty,
　So rosy and light,
Flits and is away
　As the rainbow bright,
'Tis the softest dye
　On the loveliest face,
And thrills the eye
　With a charming grace.

Vain and studied art,
　With dissembling guile,
And wicked heart
　May force a smile;
But the forced passion,
　With its silly gush,
Can ne'er fashion
　A modest blush.

HADES.

There are no more hells but Hades,
　So modern scriptorians write 'em ;
When you'd ask your friends below,
　To Hades you must invite 'em.

The devil too has lost his tail,
　Sulphur turned oleomargarine,
The blue-grass grows by the fiery lake,
　And the whole country's green ;

The ice congeals on the northern shores
　To cool its sultry hours,
Strawberries bloom on the south hill-sides
　And add perfume to the flowers ;

The orange and the lemon tree,
　The pomegranate and the grape-vine,
Blossom in perpetual spring—
　There's been a change in clime.

They've drained the bogs and the fens
　From noxious vapors free,
Killed the dragons and the snakes
　That once infested the country.

Real ice-cream and lemonade
　All o'er the land are spread,
Sparkling streams from fountains cold—
　But no more melted lead.

The dusky land of ancient gloom
 Is lit with a resplendent glow,
The ashes of its smothered fires
 Are harmless as the snow;

The ill-omened fiends with fiery eyes
 Have lost their scorpion sting,
Been transformed to fairies bright
 And taught how to sing;

Gentle zephyrs, rich with perfume
 And fraught with music rare,
Float the fleecy clouds along
 And fan the fevered air.

Oh! a glorious place this Hades,
 That supplants the realms infernal,
Curtails the devil, quenches his fires,
 And blooms in spring eternal!

As the nations still enlighten,
 And progress rolls on forever,
May they still improve old Hades—
 Old Hades across the river.

No one knows the innovations
 That 'll mark the floods of time,
The many changes in theories,
 In fancies and in rhyme.

Perhaps some enterprising theologian,
 With liberal soul and free,
Will spring a leak in old Hades yet,
 And sink 't in nonentity.

WHEN YOU AND I WERE BOYS.

They tell me, old Uncle Moses,
   Despite of all our joys,
Heaven ain't what it used to be
   When you and I were boys;
And e'en hell is changed to hades,
   That the damned may not despair,
The preachers are howling 'round,
   There's no more fire there.

The golden harp of a thousand strings
   Has half its cords broken,
And e'en our old hallelujahs
   Are by machinery spoken;
No more our swelling anthems
   Thro' all the forest ring,
But the people sit in silence
   And by hired proxy sing.

They tell us the power of prayer
   No more can reach on high,
That we are slaves to nature,
   And by nature live and die;
That Providence is but a sham,
   And hope is but a groan,
That faith is all a mystic cloud
   Covering the dark unknown;

That God, who dwelled in heaven,
   Has moved far off in space;
E'en the devil grim and sulphurous
   Ta'en to another place;

Original sin is all a fudge,
   This falling in pollution,
And man's an animal uncreate,
   Evolved by evolution.

It was not so, Uncle Moses,
   When you and I were boys,
God came down at camp-meetings
   And mingled in our joys;
The devil, like a hungry wolf,
   Sneaked 'round the camp to growl,
And ev'ry prayer sent up for grace
   Made some sinner howl.

The women then came out for prayer
   And not for inspection,
And preachers preached for the soul
   And not for the collection;
God dwelled on earth in those days,
   The church was his Zion—
The feeblest saint in all the clan
   Could choke the roaring lion.

And now 't is all for pomp and show
   The wealthy craft are tricking,
And e'en 'mong the poorest poor
   'T is old clothes and chicken;
Prayers are only made to men,
   Sermons made for cavil,
The pews are rented to the rich,
   The poor gi'n to the devil.

But, Uncle Moses, let us pray
   One of those old-fashion prayers,

And sing the songs that used to bring
God down from out the stars;
We'll bless Him for His tender love,
For life's eternal gain,
For those good old days, fore'er gone,
We'll never see again.

THE CONSULTATION.

Poor John Smith was bowed with pain,
Fever fired his blood and brain.

Sure John's was a very bad case:
His friends thought no time to waste,
So they agreed and called in consultation
Five famous doctors of the nation,
Men of experience, skilled to impart
The secret powers of the healing art,
To environ disease's vapory breath
And snatch poor John from h—l and death.
They felt his pulse, looked at his tongue,
Tasted his urine, and smelled his d—g,
Thumped his back, side, and breast,
List' to his heart, lungs, and the rest,
Took the temperature of his hide,
His secretions analyzed and magnified.

The consultation room now fairly blazes
With long, grotesque, and sonorous phrases;
What e'er tortures John might endure,
Not the least was medical nomenclature.
"'Tis very plain indeed," says Doctor A,
"We've a very simple case to-day,

As my horoscope so plainly tells,
The materies morbi is in the hepatic cells;
Perhaps a concretion is wont to mock us,
Obstructing the ductus communis choledochus."
"Tut, tut," responds the erudite B,
" 'T is conspicuous enough for me to see
The patient's liver was never at fault,
But his kidneys have sounded a halt—
Acute Bright's disease, albuminuria,
This 't is, learned confrères, I assure you."
" Just let me explain," says Doctor C,
"Then we can not fail to agree,
'T will be as plain as 't is to me
The malady is neither liver or kidney;
Had you observed closely you 'd have seen
A marked case of hypertrophied spleen ;
A masked intermittent 't is, no doubt,
Saturate with malaria in and out."
" But hold," replies our Doctor D,
" Surely you 'll all concur with me
When I 've explained my diagnosis,
'T is a case of pulmonary tuberculosis."
" Ah ! " concludes Doctor E, "a lot of asses,
To disagree 'bout such simple cases :
Just put on your spectacles and look,
'T is a plain case, cancer of the stomach,
Somewhere close in between 'em,
The pylorus and the duodenum,
Scirrhous carcinoma, not gastralgia,
Benignant ulcer or torturing neuralgia ;
As to the kidneys, liver, lungs, and spleen,
Who e'er saw them of disease so clean ?"

So this world had never known
What made poor John so howl and groan,

Had not the miserable wretch by mistake
Chanced a vial o' vermifuge to take.
The worm potion explained the situation,
And gave to all a ready explanation;
Despite the learned doctors and their terms
'T was only a simple case of worms.
Thus 't is the very learned profession,
True to an ancient popular impression,
Are tossed upon an uncertain sea,
Having agreed to simply disagree.
They live who 're saved by nature's might,
The rest are buried out of sight.
So many a poor wretch in torture squirms
Whose is a simple case of worms;
But his friends are soothed, when he reposes,
By long Greek and Latin diagnoses.

THE MONITOR.

What strange impulse, ever beating,
To my soul keeps repeating,
   Thou art immortal;
This decaying tenement of thine
But tethers thee to earth and time
   Till death break the portal?

Is it some secret thought within,
Chained by the powers of sin
   In gloomy night,
Sorrowing for the brighter days
That 'round it strewed hallow'd rays
   Of heavenly light?

Is't a monitor that would deride
The lofty flight of human pride
 O'er certain decay?
Vain creature of an uncertain hour,
With the breath that gives us power,
 Melting we pass away.

Far beyond this world's repining,
Thro' hope a brighter sphere's shining,
 Seen by our faith;
Tell us not our fancies grieve us,
That hope and faith both deceive us,
 Even in death.

Surely this strange inward feeling
Is not false, constantly revealing
 A silly part,
But from purest motives seeking
By intuition's silent speaking
 To cheer the heart.

THE AMERICAN EAGLE.

Thou, proud emblem of Liberty,
 To ev'ry American dear,
That eyries on the mountain stark
 And pinions the cloudless air,
Thou art king of the feathered tribe,
 Prince of the airy domain,
Where not a single denizen
 Disputes thy sovereign reign.

Well hast free born America
   Conceived the happy design
To emblazon the prince of birds
   Upon her eternal ensign.
Like thee, proud bird, 'mong the wilds
   She builds for Liberty a home,
Where the tempest-tossed mariner
   Can refuge from the storm;

Like thee, proud bird, she knows no peer
   In all the nations round,
Nor yet a slave in her realms,
   Lordly title nor kingly crown;
Like thee, proud bird, on pinions strong,
   When fierce tempest gathers o'er,
She wings herself above the storm
   Maddening in fury below.

As from thy rocky home, proud bird,
   Gazing on the world beneath,
America from her rock-ribbed shores
   Calmly surveys struggling earth,
Conscious of her sovereign right
   To protect each western realm,
The grandest Republic on earth
   Standing at Liberty's helm.

Proud bird, thou art an emblem true,
   In thine indomitable spirit,
Thy native courage unrestrained,
   Such only freemen inherit
From civic institutions grand,
   With no titled lord or slave,

All are freemen, and ev'ry man
His country's peerless brave.

Then build thy nest, proud bird, on high,
Preside o'er the brave and free,
Where Liberty's voice in thunder tones
Echoes o'er the land and sea ;
May thy course, proud bird, inspire
The guardians of our country's life,
Like thee, to build upon the rocks,
Far above all petty strife.

I HOLD IN TRUTH.

I hold in truth that Nature's plan
Made naught exclusively for man,
Nothing solely for his uses,
For his pride or his abuses ;
The generous laws that give him health
Spread for all a bounteous wealth,
The source from whence he draws his food
Is pabulum for the menial brood,
The flesh on which his limbs repair
Feeds likewise the tiger and the bear,
The grain that feeds his thinking brain
Gives voice to nightingale or crane.
Throughout life's mysterious way
The stronger on the weaker prey,
Which in turn to still stronger yield,
For murder's rife on ev'ry field,
And man himself, howe'er he squirms,
Is only food for crawling worms.

I hold in truth, tho' none applaud,
This world's filled with many a fraud;
Society's artificial at least,
And man an educated beast.
In ages past, when Time was young,
Ere man had found a tuneful tongue,
Or language of deceitful guile,
He wandered thro' the jungles wild,
To forest dark or caverns deep
At night he retired to sleep,
Disputed with the wolf and bear
The shelter of each dusky lair,
But not so proud or yet so blind
To scorn the kinship of his kind,
Contended with the various beast,
From the strongest e'en to the least;
Tho' often worsted still he thrived,
And as the fittest of all survived.

I hold in truth, of firm accord,
Nature made man—Nature is God;—
Man made society, priest, and kings,
And all the host of titled things
Who hold their's the fruits of earth
By rights divine or privileged birth.

I hold that thro' all nature wide
There flows of blood one common tide,
Thro' man, thro' beast, thro' all creatures,
Elements the same in changing features.

I hold that, from creation's birth,
Through all the ages of the earth,
Where struggling nature still survives,
The dead live on in other lives;

Though wasted by dissolving storms
Their elements still seek new forms—
And all this but at trifling cost,
The identity is only lost,
However fast these changes be,
They begin and end in eternity,
Where Nature its own bosom warms
And God breathes life in all its forms.

I hold in truth, firmly resolved,
From rude barbarity evolved
Came man, crude, ignorant, and wild,
Companion of beast, Nature's child—
Experience was his education;
Thence the family, thence the nation,
Formed at first for mutual defense,
Then favored ones found opulence—
Opulence, ease—ease lead to pride,
Then flung society's gates wide;
Wealth, ease, and pride all lead to caste,
Hence our kings, lords, prophets, and priest.
Through all the races of mankind
A few have ruled the world with mind;
The lowly herds in serfdom blind,
Enslaved by rights presumed divine,
Are bound in superstition's chains
To kingly rights and priestly manes;
They labor in incessant toil,
While others fatten on their spoil.

I hold in truth, of proud degree,
Man is yet in his infancy,
Even the wisest of our time
Can boast no more than manhood's prime,

The mature wisdom of the sage
Will come to yet an unborn age.
In my prophetic eye I trace
Banished from earth ev'ry disgrace,
And king and priest and menial herd
All to a barbarous age referred;
But 'bove fanaticism and might
Stand human equality and right,
Defenders of our destiny,
Twin brothers of our liberty,
Intelligence sheds 'broad its light,
And men do right for sake of right!
Then virtue is its own reward,
More potent than a tyrant's sword;
No visions of the silver spheres
Allure men from human cares,
Nor roaring hells in grim pretense
Shock either modesty or sense,
No conscience educated base
To bow serf to a brother race,
But as free in mind as in birth,
Survives the fittest of the earth.

MUSINGS.

Is life real, or are we dreaming
    In this strange, strange world?
Is thought just as 't is seeming
    In its ever busy whirl,
Or are we but fleeting shadows
    Cast on the dial of time,

Simply to index the passage
  Of nature's laws sublime?

When we peer into the darkness,
  Eternity that has been,
Where were our dusky shadows,
  Had we existence then?
Who has looked into the future
  In the ages to come?
Who has seen a soul immortal
  In its great spirit home?

Dark the clouds of revelation,
  Dark the benighted slave
Who turns from science and reason
  To priestcraft's slimy grave;
Yet 't is not science or learning,
  'T is not reason's control,
But a confidence eternal
  In the immortal soul.

Is he an impious infidel,
  Dead to all nobler deeds,
Who can not link God Almighty
  With factions and their creeds?
Is he a fiend of black darkness,
  Has he the faith denied,
Who scorns a vile arrant priesthood
  In its deceitful pride?

Then let me be that infidel!
  Oh! let me be that fiend
Who has for God a higher rev'rence,
  For man a brighter dream,

Who scorns all fanaticisms
　　Nor bows to priestly guiles,
Whose faith and hope is God alone,
　　Not sacerdotal smiles!

My secret soul, be not depressed,
　　Thrive on what reason gives,
Read from the lessons of the heart,
　　God still in nature lives—
In nature lives, in reason lives,
　　In evidence most bright,
His golden sun with radiant rays
　　Dispelling cloudy night.

BIRDS OF A FEATHER.

The geese cackle loudly
　　For the gander of the flock,
Scorning the noble eagle
　　That perches on the rock;
Thus the human bipeds
　　Are oft loudest heard
When they'd praise the feathers
　　Of a kindred bird.

So votaries of a creed
　　File where leaders meander,
Cackling like silly geese
　　To compliment the gander;
The loftiest intellects,
　　Towering like mountain rocks,

Are scorned simply because
They are of other flocks.

The geese smile audibly,
With rev'rence and respect,
To hear the old gander
In goosely dialect;
So e'en 'mong quadrupeds,
The pride of caste's display,
The jennets think it's music
When the jackasses bray.

The mother dotes on her child,
And thinks its silly prattle
But the golden blossom
Prospective of the mettle;
No difference how foolish,
How wretched or deformed,
No brighter intellect
Nor fairer bosom warmed.

Who preaches innovation
Is but a civic thief,
No excellence but the present
In practice or belief;
In politics or religion,
In life's contending shocks,
The music streams only
From organs orthodox.

THE FALLEN.

Deal gently with a fallen sister,
  You may never know
The feelings of deep contrition
  That fill her life with woe;
Sad, sad lessons of experience
  Wring the soul with pain,
Deeply scarred the human heart
  With virtue's improvident stain.

One glance of scornful reproach
  The ties of hope may sever,
And deeper into human woe
  Drive the soul forever;
One word of sweet sympathy,
  A cheering look unspoken,
May stay an erring one
  And heal a heart's broken.

When human folly fills its cup,
  'Tis indeed with bitter grief
Wayward fancy sips its draught,
  Repenting tears bring no relief;
One rash act imbues the stain,
  Heaven alone heeds repenting,
Tears fall on hearts of stone,
  Society is unrelenting.

Virtue once from truth decoyed,
  Lives only by natural mights,
Confidence but once destroyed
  Estranges all society's rights;
8

Whate'er motives might inspire,
 Fore'er stamped on life and time
Is passion's foul desire
 And bloody stains of crime.

You know not the bitter thoughts
 That tremble in the heart
Contending with the human soul
 And passion's cruel dart;
You know not the secret tears,
 Shed o'er folly's unhallow'd graves,
When conscience with scorpions lash
 Its miscreant slaves.

Deal gently with an erring sister,
 Perhaps to you 't is given
To save a life to usefulness
 And a soul to heaven;
If you'd have an easy conscience
 When eternity's cycles swell,
If you can not lift the fallen,
 Do not push them into hell.

MY LIFE, MY LOVE.

My life, my love, my dream, my joy!
 All my earthly treasure,
As sweet as honey from the comb,
 The joys of stolen pleasure;
Let others boast the marital couch,
 Its sameness and repose,
The bee gathers sweets for his hive
 From violet and rose.

Free as the bees that kiss the breath
  From ev'ry bud and flower,
We'll wander by field and wood,
  Nor count the fleeting hour;
'T is society that frowns or smiles,
  'T is custom that disgraces,
Nature's love's as pure and sweet
  As Hymen's own embraces.

The law may bind with iron bands
  Souls that are sick with grief,
Love's no bonds but tenderest cords
  And sues for no relief;
Tell me not the love's impure
  That needs no chain to bind it,
That heaven has ne'er sealed a vow
  Without a priest behind it.

Too oft the vows society demands,
  And takes without discretion,
Make marriage bonds but prison chains
  To youth's mistaken passion;
Too oft the rights we call divine
  The marriage bed disgraces,
Where hearts of ice fulfill their vows
  And meet in cold embraces.

Love should be free and unrestrained
  To seek its own findings,
Nor think the looseness of the cords
  Less sacred to the bindings;
Where hearts throb warm in mutual love,
  The union is eternal,
Unwilling hearts are chained by law,
  The union is infernal.

MEET ME, LOVE.

Oh! meet me, Love, beside the wood,
    Let us renew our vows and praise,
There lingers 'round our trysting place
    The memories of other days;
Where 'neath the shadows of the tree,
    Where blooms the violet and rose,
We've whispered in each other's ears
    What loving hearts alone disclose.

Beside the spring, all moss o'er-grown,
    Cling the grape-vines to the trees,
The songs of birds, perfumes of flowers
    Make redolent ev'ry breeze;
How sweet the spring, how sweet the birds,
    How sweet the memories of the day!
The trees, the vines, the leaves, the flowers,
    Combine to chase all cares away.

Now memories back their steps retrace,
    Fondly review each scene again,
Where pleasure twines 'round ev'ry hour,
    And only parting gives us pain;
Should we meet e'en now, my Love,
    'T would but wake anew the smarting,
The winged hours so quick would flee,
    Grief 'd return again at parting.

Still there's a power within me robs
    My heart and soul of ev'ry rest,
I chase the moments for their joys
    As birds from off a hidden nest;

When they would lead me from their homes
  They fall and flutter at my feet,
I stretch my hand to grasp the prize,
  But 't is gone—well-feigned deceit.

Such are the secret hopes of love
  That 'lure the soul but to despair,
They flee like phantoms 'fore the chase,
  Which ere you grasp dissolve in air;
Ah! such the hopes of all this life
  Which men pursue but ne'er control,
But hope itself's a child of Love,
  Dies only with the human soul.

Then meet me, Love, but once again,
  The same sweet smile upon your face,
And I will kiss the tears away
  That come at our parting embrace;
Let hell invent its direst woes
  And try to turn my joy to grief,
My heart will feast upon that hour
  And in its memory find relief.

COME, MY LOVE.

Come, my Love, when the Vespers wane,
Though our parting gives us pain,
While the blissful moments last
We'll ne'er repine o'er the past;
Let me but gaze into your eyes,
From whence the loving glances rise,
Read in the azured depths beneath
Endearing thoughts the heart would sheath.

Come, Love, lean on my yearning breast,
Come steal your arms around my waist.
Oh! let me drink, as the bee sips,
The nectar from thy honeyed lips.
Ye gods! in truth, and this is love
Drawn from Elysian founts above,
Here Narcissus with abated breath
Could pine over the form beneath.

Come, Love, with your thousand charms,
Let me press you in my arms,
As my soul desires to please you,
To my heaving bosom squeeze you;
Wipe ev'ry tear from out your eyes
And kiss away all troubling sighs,
Read in your very look the token,
Words of love before they're spoken.

Let your throbbing heart beat kindly,
As I've loved you madly, blindly,
Loved you with the wildest passion,
Loved you with thoughtless discretion,
Loved you, whate'er fate betide you,
Loved you with your faults beside you,
Whate'er the world might say or make,
Loved you for your own sweet sake.

Let us ne'er dream of the parting,
Of its heartache and its smarting,
Let the now be the forever,
Which no cruel fate can sever,
That we may not repine the past
While the joyous moments last,
Nor cloud to-day with to-morrow—
Living bliss with unborn sorrow.

Come then, Darling, to the meeting
With the sweetest smiles of greeting—
Smiles as soft, as sweet, endearing,
As love whispers to the hearing;
I've a secret for your ears, Love,
It'll drive away your fears, Love,
I've a hundred fond embraces
And a thousand honeyed kisses.

Come, my Love, when the Vespers wane,
Tho' our parting give us pain,
While the blissful moments last
We'll ne'er repine o'er the past;
In my arms I will fold you,
In my heart an idol mold you,
By all the living gods divine,
I'll worship at no other shrine!

SING ME A SONG OF LOVE.

Oh! sing to me a song of love,
　My heart is filled with grief;
Love 'wakes the tend'rest cords of life,
　And brings the soul relief.

Oh! sing to me of home and friends,
　With glad, smiling faces,
Clinging in to our bosoms warm
　With a thousand embraces.

Oh! sing to me of children sweet,
　With golden locks of hair,
Gathering 'round the mother's knee,
　As artless as they're fair.

Oh! sing to me of youth's bright hours,
    Awake its memories dear,
Those Elysian hours passed and gone,
    Unstained by sorrow's tear.

Oh! sing to me the lullabies
    That soothed my childish fear
When I slept on my mother's breast
    Unknown to any care;   .

But sing no more the songs that fright
    The soul from reveries sweet,
That fling the shadowy forms of death
    'Round pleasure's moment fleet.

Oh! sing no more the woes of life,
    No more its battle's cry,
But strew sweet flowers o'er ev'ry plain—
    There let us live and die.

FOOLS.

Some natural fools as fools are born,
    Some fools by occupation,
The worst fools that disgrace mankind,
    Are fools by education;
'Tis hard to tell where wisdom end
    And where the fool begins,
But beware when self-abasements
    Are added to your sins.

Kings recline on beds of flowers,
    A priest behind each throne,
And while the twain feast to fatness
    The toiling millions groan;

The kings, the earls, the dukes, the lords,
  And priests of all the schools,
Would have to learn some other trade
  If 't was not for the fools.

The fools hew wood and water draw,
  They make the anvils ring,
To put power and wealth on mitred heads
  And purple on the king;
But reason dawns upon the earth,
  Let mankind observe its rules,
All rights divine of king or priest
  Are but to enslave the fools.

WOMAN.

Oh! what will we say for our women
  When the evil days do come;
Hope departs from the bosom of man
  To find with woman a' home;
When our minds are weighed down with sorrow
  And our souls are draped with night,
We turn from the gloom of a fainting heart
  And look to our women for light.
Women, the sun of all our hopes,
  The bright dawn that forecasts the morrow,
Nature's balm for the wounded heart,
  A surcease from sickness and sorrow;
Let us love our women, and cherish
  All the goodness her nature imparts,
Nor distrust the truth or sweets of her love
  Transplanted like a rose in our hearts.

KNOW THOU NOT?

Know thou not one truth at least,
While you fast the preachers feast?
Never dream God may be bribed
With penance by a church prescribed;
The rival churches undismayed,
In bloody feuds were long arrayed,
In peace their holiest relations
Are only jealous tolerations.
The priests, in truth, have ne'er agreed
Among themselves on any creed,
But have quarreled, like dogs and cats,
O'er cut of hair or shape of hats,
And oaths as hot as hell have sent
O'er ev'ry faith and sacrament;
None e'er denied but that 't was right
With sword and stake to proselyte,
Provided only the scourging rods
Were of their faith and of their gods;
Murder is right when for the creed,
But dire enough when disagreed
Whether, 'neath crescent in the east
Or under cross of Christian priest,
With fire and sword the righteous strong
Condemn the weaker, right or wrong.
The slogan cry of ev'ry sect,
Whatever priest or god direct,
With heretic blood be meekness crammed—
Believe with us, or you'll be d——d.

THE MARTYRS.

Light your faggots, burn the martyrs,
 Men of wisdom and of right!
For the flames that leap around them
 Will dispel the coming night;
Curse them for each innovation,
 Like fiends still hunt them down;
With mighty nations yet unborn,
 They'll be the glory of our own.

They are men who've dared thro' death
 To guide man's erring soul aright,
And from the red flames of the stake
 Point to truth's golden light.
Onward is the march of progress;
 The great man lives before his time
To die in shame, tho' coming ages
 Resurrect his name sublime.

Brave men explore the tides of passion,
 Like frail bark out at sea,
Among the breakers and the rocks
 They chart a path for you and me;
Denying self and self-ambition,
 Leading where conscience points the right,
Despising dungeons, swords, and flame,
 To bequeath to us the light.

Sun of Reason, thou art dawning,
 From thy shining quiver dart
Rays of truth, dispelling darkness
 From the human soul and heart,
Till man's free, unfettered conscience
 Measures truth and measures sage,
And proscription cease forever
 From the glory of the age.

NATURE'S LAWS.

He who nature's laws disgraces
To his heart a dagger places,
God Almighty ne'er effaces
 Nature's laws.

O! ye who so weakly languish
On beds of disease and anguish,
'T is because God can't extinguish
 Nature's laws.

Till heaven and earth pass away
And matter back to chaos stray,
Omniscient wisdom ne'er can stay
 Nature's laws.

We live by Nature's own respect,
We die as nature may direct,
All our actions circumspect
 Nature's laws.

Changeless as the Eternal Mind,
Unswerving as the sunbeams shine,
Life respects in ev'ry design
 Nature's laws.

Happy he who may early learn,
From truth and wisdom to discern,
And in life's broad way ne'er to spurn
 Nature's laws.

OUR DAYS FOR FUN ARE O'ER, JIM.

Our days for fun are o'er, Jim,
 Those merry days of yore,
When out among the girls

We pulled their pretty curls,
Then life in joyous whirls
  Had charms for every hour.

Our days for fun are o'er, Jim,
  They come to us no more ;
A thousand joys untold,
All cast in pleasure's mold,
Moments dearer than gold,
  The world can ne'er restore.

Our days for fun are o'er, Jim,
  We are growing older,
Tot'ring in life and limb,
Our eyes are ageing dim,
We are on the ragged brim—
  Life is daily colder.

Our days for fun are o'er, Jim,
  The friends we used to know,
With whom in life we started,
One by one have parted,
And almost unhearted
  We are waiting to follow.

Our days for fun are o'er, Jim,
  And sorrows all surround ;
But why need we to weep?
What has this life to keep?
Where our companions sleep
  We 'll lay our burdens down.

THE SEASONS.

Now the glad spring,
  With joyous peal,
Its mantle flings
  O'er wood and field ;

And nature smiles
  The live long day,
The heart beguiles
  In ev'ry way.

Then the summer
  With genial showers,
A welcome comer
  To our bowers;
It charms our dreams
  With sparkling rills,
Where pour cool streams
  From shady hills.

The autumn mature,
  With yellow leaf,
Dismantles nature
  Like as a thief.
Why need we start,
  Are we so blind,
Is not the heart
  Thus scared by time?

Our hearts are warm,
  Tho' drear forecasts
The bitter storm
  Of winter's blasts;
We too must find
  A winter rife,
Where ice-chains bind
  The streams of life.

The flow'ry spring
  Is infant time,
The summers bring
  Manhood to prime,
The autumns mature
  Wisdom's fair sage,

Winter is nature
Frosty with age.

Oh! may we learn,
While yet in youth,
To e'er discern
Nature's own truth;
He 'll find in wrath
Sore repentance,
Who dares to laugh
At experience.

TO THOS. PAINE.

Thos. Paine, the friend of Liberty,
Thos. Paine, the tried and true,
Struck with might and struck with courage
For the rights to freemen due,
Broke the chains of regal slavery,
Drove the church and state abort;
Common Sense and Age of Reason
Dawned upon the human heart.

He broke society's inquisition,
Scattered proscription's faggots,
Marked the bloody and slimy trail
Of priestly worms and maggots;
Struck truth and right from cringing faith,
And many a mind he freed,
Whose soul expands in the light of day,
Unfettered by mystic creed.

Truth 's eternal and will survive,
Tho' the powers of hell conspire,

'T will spring from the grave of martyrs,
'T will live through blood and fire;
You may tread 't to earth and crush it,
You may scatter it o'er the main,
Deeply sown in the hearts of men,
'T will spring in life again.

Reason's the sun of Liberty,
True sovereign of all the earth,
Kings and priests may call it treason
And attempt to crush its birth,
But it will break the dungeon bars
In every king's dominion,
And quench the priestly fires of hate
That burn men for opinion.

Thos. Paine, champion of Truth,
The great apostle of the free,
Nations yet unborn will wreath
The glory of his memory;
And though we've laid his dust away,
Heaped with calumny and strife,
Despite the howl of savage priest
We'll live his lessons of life.

His noble words are not forgotten,
His courage strong as iron,
When the struggling colonies
Cowed 'neath the British Lion;
'T was him first said, "Let us be free,
All men 're equal by birth;"
His glorious words will yet outring
The dastard howl of priestly dearth.

MODERN JUSTICE.

They say that Justice is really blind,
Not with good eyes a bandage behind,
Yet her ancient and trusty scales
Now oft upon the balance fails;
As to her sword, for vengeance trusted,
The point's blunt, the edge is rusted;
Dead is her ally, Common Sense,
Killed by technical evidence.

If Justice be blind, the old "galoot"
Leads like a sow ringed in the "snoot;"
Tho' she be lame, decrepid, and old,
She still smiles at the sound of gold,
Sometimes rising in bristling might
To strike an impecunious wight;
The rich, who for immunity've paid,
Ne'er feel the fury of her blade.

Justice, once blind to extraneous hints,
Is blind no more—she only squints,
Opes her eyes to all that's before,
Shuts them in time to strike the poor;
The rich from kleptomania steal,
Kill, and to insanity appeal—
These are aristocratic stains,
Such blood courses not plebeian veins.

Poor Vonderhide! the devil take him!
No friends or money to back him,
Made an example for coming time,
Forfeits his neck to rid his crime.
Jim Arnold and Tom Buford bold,
Fiends of murder most foul and cold;

9

Money appeals to humanity,
Self-defense, or at least insanity.

Lawyers, despite their vaunting boast,
Are but priest to this haggard ghost,
Tickling vanity for her smiles;
Old Justice is pleased with their guiles,
Sits on her throne, dull as a snail,
While they fix the weights in her scale,
Or, if she can not be delayed,
Impose a shield before her blade.

Tho' old, and wrinkled in complexion,
Justice'll do for an election,
E'en the nation may feel her sword
When 't champions a Returning Board;
Three carpet-baggers, hearty and hale,
Outweighed Louisiana in her scale;
Justice, in high mockery instated,
Struck as party guile dictated.

A FABLE.

Assembled in convocation,
Beast and varmints of the nation,
Thought to determine by debate
A question of religion or state;
A wise old owl, judge-like, umpired.
Some for Bumbcome were inspired;
Many opinions had a hearing,
Divers theories got an airing,
When nicest points in logic turned
The arguments were grave and learned;
Those who no thought themselves possessed

Fiercely criticised all the rest.
'T was hard to tell, so poised each side,
Which way the umpire would decide,
Till the jackass, smiling sedate,
Calmly 'rose to end the debate ;
Back fell the varmints all dismayed,
For loud and long the savant brayed,
Foamed and pawed with bellow and shout
Till every sound was drowned out.
Then said they all with one agree,
'' Surely the ass has the victory."
" Hold," said the owl, " in howl and bray,
The ass has truly won the day ;
But not with reason he employs.
With least of wit he 's most of noise."

The same in truth may well be said
Of Nature's great unfledged biped ;
His lungs to task are oft' exacted
When his brain is most contracted,
While modest worth may hide away
What 's louder than an ass's bray.

A FABLE, NO. 2.

An old she-bear with two proud cubs
Which dwelt among the mountain shrubs,
Secure in her lonely retreat,
Her lair untread by hunter's feet,
Thought of some plan she might devise,
Some secret scheme, goodly and wise,
To keep her cubs out the valley
Where the hunters' clans did rally.

The wayward cubs, with head-strong will,
Had no fear of huntsman's skill,
Tho' they were told the human kind
The rights of beast could never find.
Savage varmints on men do feast,
The best of men may slay the beast.
Primeval man with naked sense
Hardly lived by self defense;
Since he's formed himself in nations
He's got 'bove his old relations,
With flint and club his own he held,
But modern arms are made too well.
The old she-bear knew of the skill
Powder and steel gave man to kill,
So in her heart she framed a lie
To cheat her wayward children by;
She told them, "In the neighboring glen
Dwelled an evil worse than men—
A monstrous form lived in a cave,
Where truant cubs would find a grave;"
This served her purpose, for the bear
Restrained the cubs safe in her lair.
Thus the mother, shrewd and wary,
Wards true danger with imaginary;
And so the immortal beast we find
E'en reason as his mortal kind,
With Devil of his own invention
He tries to serve a good intention.
Where real virtue fails to charm,
This spectral ghost makes an alarm.
And here's the paradox forsooth—
Falsehood becomes the food of truth;
If truth itself was always good,
A lie could never serve it food.

THE CHASE BY NIGHT.

When the evening sun had faded
　From the waning afternoon,
And the soft shadows were creeping
　With the rising of the moon,
The good dogs danced to the music
　And the bugle was in tune.

Down through the gloomy hollow
　And over the craggy hills,
With bugle blast and clamoring hounds,
　When evening winds were still
And moon and stars from out the sky
　Reflected from every rill,

The red fox sprang from his lair,　　　'
　Shook himself and was away;
Our trusty friends scent his trail,
　They 'll chase him till the day.
Oh! there was music in the air,
　And the blithe hunters were gay.

Soft and mellow floated the strain,
　The air unruffled by a gale;
Old Towse was far before the pack
　And the first to strike the trail,
We 'd have heard his shrill clarion voice
　If every other voice fail.

And now another strikes the note,
　And yet another still,
Until an hundred voices seem
　All the wood and field to fill,
And every rock and cavern 'round
　Prolonged the joyous thrill.

As we listened to the baying,
  We marked by each changing sound
When our good dogs were gaining,
  When they were losing ground;
And with bugle chorused the clamor,
  And cheered the fainting hound.

But hark! the chase is thick'ning now,
  The fox is wearying fast;
Now spur your steed, ye huntsmen true,
  Let ditch and fence be passed,
If ye'd be in at the killing
  Ere reynard breathes his last.

TO THOS. CARLYLE.

Thou grim Lion of Chelsea,
  Before whom the literati pale,
On cold philosophy fed,
Has no inward light been shed
Upon thy chilly heart
  To soften its iron mail?

Why does the world regard thee
  Like a monster in his cage?
As if the darksome storm
That keeps thy bosom warm
Was the lightning's flash
  Or the thunder's rage.

Like some craggy rock
  On snowy clift towering high,

Above the genial smiling earth,
'Bove men of ordinary birth,
Thou standeth as 'mid clouds
  Capped by the azured sky.

Woe to human follies,
  When thy piercing eagle eye
Looks from beneath its shaggy brow
Upon the earth teeming below,
'T is as the lightning's flash
  From out a stormy sky.

Still we think 'neath the rugged rocks
  A rougher nature rears;
In the heart is a warmer spring,
Where affections yet fondly cling,
Falling softly on human grief
  Like a fond mother's tears.

But what now is fame to thy age,
  Feebly tottering on the grave!
Thy mind can never try again
The fire of its youthful strain;
Thou who once was Nature's prince,
  Art now but Nature's slave.

But not so much what thou art
  As what thou hast been,
When manhood in stately prime
But indexed thy nobler mind,
We bow before thee, revered sage,
  A sovereign prince of men.

ON THE DEATH OF A FRIEND.

Cruel is fate, and unkind,
　Thus to torture my rest,
To madden my frenzied mind
　And tear my bleeding breast.
Has heaven ne'er a feeling
　For the sad heart's relief,
To see me madly kneeling
　In agony and grief?

Are bereavements ne'er so deep
　Oblivions may attend,　　　　　·
As bright angels in the sleep
　Of those they would befriend,
Soothing the sad heart's aching
　With balm from sunny clime,
When our grieved souls are breaking
　On the rough wheel of time?

The fairest flower that casts
　Its tender blossom forth
Withers before the fierce blast
　Streaming from out the north;
So, 'mid this world's seething strife,
　Disease's vapory breath,
The loveliest forms of life
　Are marked by cruel death.

Those we've learned to know and love,
　Idolize their actions,
Are singled out from above
　And torn from our affections;
Bitter experience imparts
　Sad lesssons night and day,

The idols of the human heart
  Are only things of clay.

Oh! who has not lost one dear,
  Who has not heard the groan,
When the Fates unkindly tear
  Loved ones from the hearth-stone?
Who has not felt the sad care
  O'er his soul strangely shed,
Gazing on the empty chair
  Shadow'd by recent dead?

We stand by a lonely grave
  Solemnly and profound,
Eternity's chilly wave
  Dashes with muffled sound;
We strain to catch an echo
  From out its hollow cave,
Silently the waters flow—
  No response from the grave.

We ask the fields and mountains,
  We ask the cloudy sky,
We ask ocean's deepest fountains,
  In vain for a reply.
Hast thou seen our friend, the dead,
  In the far spirit spheres?
Hast thou e'er heard his soft tread,
  Silent to human ears?

Still we linger 'round his tomb
  With mingled hopes and fears;
Perhaps, from out its dark gloom,
  He smiles upon our tears,
Or with extended arm stands,
  Smiling at all our cares,
Pointing to the better lands
  Beyond our dusky spheres.

10

THE TORNADO.

I stood where the forest was dark
  With the shadow of the storm,
And beheld the fierce tornado
  As it madly swept along
Like some hideous monster wild,
  Breathing destruction and death;
The thunders roared his angry voice,
  The lightnings flamed his breath;

The noise of his advancing tread
  Was like the clash of mettle
When fiercest hordes in mad array
  Rush wildly to battle;
Before him in incessant flames
  The sheeted lightnings raced,
Behind the groaning thunders roared
  'Mid forest's broken waste;

The tallest oaks shivered and flew,
  Twisted by whirlwinds with ease,
As lightly as a thistle down
  Borne by summer's gentlest breeze.
When the destruction had passed by,
  Rolling as on fiery wheels,
I gazed upon the scattered wreck
  As on a thousand battle fields.

The clouds whirled in wild confusion
  High 'bove the hurricane's path,
Like the boiling of smoke and flame
  Above a volcano's wrath;
And on it came in fury wild,
  Dragging a dire train behind,

With death and hell in every breath,
  Most awfully sublime.

The men rushed madly from their homes,
  The wild beast from out each lair,
The birds, screaming with awful fright,
  Whirled 'round with the circling air ;
Over hills and dales widely strown
  The mangled dead and dying,
And scarce the rocks and mountains firm
  The fierce tempest defying.

THE FALLEN.

When woman in all her beauty
Strangely forgets th' sacred duty
Her heart must ever be true to
  To reap virtue's rewards,

And with a bold and brazen face
Blushes not at the foul disgrace
That severs her from all the race
  Of modest womankind,

All her lovely charms are faded.
Is moral darkness deeper shaded,
Is human wretch e'er more degraded
  In society's mind ?

Woman, we love and adore her,
All our hopes are hovered o'er her,
But what power can restore her
  When once she has fallen ?

Perhaps a pure love misplaced,
A frailty of the human race,

And yet the stain can't be effaced
　By oceans of tears.

Perhaps it was but the heeding
Of a faithless lover's pleading,
Who left her soul and heart bleeding
　With confidence betrayed.

Few, few indeed of woman's name,
Who have stooped to sin and shame,
On whom alone will rest the blame
　When heaven avenges?

Wretched woman, thy tear-stained groan
May reach heaven's pitying throne,
But mortal man will cast the stone—
　Himself unforgiven.

JOHN BUNYAN.

John Bunyan was a sickly saint,
　Put in prison madly,
His Christian had the dyspepsia,
　And had it very badly,
Hence when John wrote for moral good
　He wrote very sadly;
Now, if you'd have his epitaph,
　I will pen it gladly:

Here lies John Bunyan, doubly blessed,
May his soul and body rest;
If only sour saints get to glory,
His will be an upper story.

THE SNEAK.

I dread not the fierce lion
  Nor tiger in my pass,
But I dread the sneaking snake
  That lurks in the grass;
The lion may be savage,
  The tiger true as steel,
Only the snake in the grass
  Will bite you in the heel.

There's a high nobility
  In every honest foe
Who meets you bravely, boldly,
  And strikes an open blow;
Not from secret ambuscade,
  Not from coverts stark,
With assassin's stealthy steps
  From hidden caverns dark.

He's a cowardly dastard,
  But seeking your disgrace,
Who, frowning behind your back,
  Smiles sweetly to your face;
Give me an open enemy,
  One worthy of my steel,
Save me from the sneaking cur
  That snarls at my heel.

Behind a deceitful smile
  With venomous guile o'ergrown,
The sneak plays a murderous part
  And strikes with hand unknown;
He greets you e'er so friendly,
  Subtle fawning no lack;

Beware! when you least expect it,
   He'll stab you in the back.

Show me the true gentleman,
   Who acts a brave man's part,
Who measures swords on equal ground
   With an undaunted heart ;
Be he your friend or your foe,
   You need no vigils keep,
He 'll never steal upon you
   And strike you in your sleep.

Show me the sneaking coward,
   With his dissembling air,
He's lurking with stealthy step
   To strike you unaware ;
Beware the two-faced villain,
   Watch him whene'er he pass,
He 's a cur behind your back,
   He 's a snake in the grass.

TALK ABOUT THE GOLDEN SLIPPERS.

Talk about the golden slippers
   Which bright angels wear,
There are but few mortal toes
   That can squeeze in a pair,
Tho' grace with sacerdotal shears
   Trim their corns with care.

Many a heart, relentless, proud,
   Ne'er sipped temptation's gall,
Nor passed with feet all bare and sore
   Where oft' the bravest fall,

Free from the seductive passions
  That weaker men inthrall.

Ah! could ye see the bitter woe
  Pressed to unwilling lips,
Tho' the soul may loathe its power
  But yet enslaved it sips,
Spell-bound to the poisonous cup
  That with damnation drips.

Has humanity yet no tears
  To shed o'er his disgrace?
Has Christianity no prayers,
  In all its stock of grace,
For the man with soul immortal
  Whose passions have no peace?

Oh! ye who boast victories divine
  O'er temptations untried,
Ye've never known the bitter strife
  Of some whom you deride;
Virtuous souls battling for right,
  A fouler flesh belied.

AFTER THE BATTLE.

The enemy have fled, the battle it is o'er—
The cannons' thunder, the rifles' incessant roar,
The charge and the retreat amid dismay and wrath,
And bursting of fiery shells 'long their murderous path.

The clouds are clearing 'way from off the bloody field,
Where the victors exult and the vanquished yield,
Where in sick'ning carnage the mangled and the slain,
The dead and the dying, are scattered o'er the plain.

Here in ghastly heaps our bravest sons fell,
When the battle-field shook with canister and shell;
From the rifle-pits, stubborn and undismayed,
A leaden death rained on every charge made;

Solid shot and shell, grape-shot and chain,
Furrowed thro' the columns, but they closed again;
Still onward they charged, death and hell defying,
The battle's roar drowning the groans of the dying.

As we gaze o'er the field where dead and wounded lie,
Many a strange scene greets the unhappy eye,
Many a bitter groan fills the heart with grief,
The mangled in anguish are pleading for relief.

Here among the dead, and who will weep no more,
A flaxen-haired boy lies chilled in his gore;
One hand upon his heart tells of a nobler rest,
The other clasps a Bible to his bosom pressed.

And here lies one alone, where sympathy may start,
Kneeling as if a prayer was bubbling from his heart;
Close beside him a missive, softer than the strife—
It told of tender loves of children, home, and wife.

And here lies another, a gray-haired sire,
His eyes blood-shot with frenzy's maddening ire,
With an oath on his lips, his heart in passion burned,
He fell on the rifle-pits when waning victory turned.

Many a mother's heart, beating strangely and wild,
Hears the battle's roar, praying for her child;
Comrades will tell, no doubt, his was the bravest part,
And this ghost of glory must soothe the mother's heart.

Mother and child, when they hear the night-winds humming,
Will rush to the door to see if father is coming;

When he comes no more, others will tell the story,
Lone widow and orphan—this, my friends, is glory.

O! ye who thirst for fame, here her victims are spread;
Come hear their dying groans, come and see the dead
Heaped in many ghastly heaps, mangled and gory.
This indeed is fame, and this her field of glory.

HOWEVER DEEP IN SIN AND STRIFE.

However deep in sin and strife
    Man's lead by misdirection,
There are some hours in every life
    Of sober reflection.

No heart so hard, so like a stone,
    So filled with human cares,
But that at times 't is melted down
    And softened into tears.

However low fallen in sin,
    By human folly driven,
There is in man something akin
    To his pristine heaven.

Let them rave who are wont to teach
    Depravity is total,
And naught but faith in priest can reach
    Beyond the grim portal.

Oh! judge ye not man by his faith,
    But rather by his deeds;
The purest men who 've lived on earth
    Are damned by all the creeds.

Who heeds the mandates of his breast
  No evil can betide,
The conscience that can bring its rest
  Is the noblest guide.

Why talk of faith to hungry men,
  Why burden them with creeds!
Go feed the poor, the sick attend,
  Go succor human needs!

ANGELS' VISITS.

When slumber's soft chain my weary limbs binds,
  There comes to me in the shadows of night,
As fair as the day ere the eve declines,
  A being of love transcendently bright.

She moves in my chamber, soft as the light
  That fades from the brow of declining day,
As a fairy would move on moonbeams bright,
  Softer than the dew-drops that round her stray;

She leans o'er my couch with a smile serene,
  She whispers in my ears a tale of love.
I 'wake from my sleep and I think 't is a dream,
  Nor know 't is a visit from angels above;

Then I close my eyes and I dream a prayer,
  And I feel soft lips to my own lips pressed,
A heavenly odor pervading the air
  As one on a couch of flowers did rest.

Oh! the sweet visions that pass thro' my mind
  And float away on the tide of my dreams,
Like the evening clouds when the summer's wind
  Drifts them in life forms and gilds them with beams.

I commune in my sleep with the spirits of peace,
  My soul is filled with heavenly delight,
And soothed my conscience reposes at ease
  As rests the earth 'neath the shades of night.

IF MAN DIES, SHALL HE LIVE AGAIN?

Why ask this question of the soul?
What secret torch 's at man's soul,
Streaming its light o'er life's dark plain,
To tell us if man lives again?

Do the desires of the heart,
The soul's anguish or secret smart,
Answer the longings of the mind
And surely sight the hopeless blind?

Then is there light in every breast,
And should be peace, content, and rest?
For what bosom is without faith,
And hope in life beyond the death? ·

Who doubts Nature's powers to give
The future life we hope to live?
Why make the heart a barren plain
And plant a hope that blooms in vain?

Whence came this dream, if 't is a dream,
Where hope blossoms forever green?
What spirit awoke these visions strange,
So far beyond man's mental range?

Yes, we all trust, but do not know,
We fondly hope, but are not sure,
That life's longings are not in vain,
And tho' man dies, he'll live again.

THE SUNNY SOUTHLAND.

All hail! the American Eagle,
　　All hail! the illustrious brave,
Who love the ensign of stars and stripes
　　Wherever its colors wave.
Who will blame my pride of section?
　　The Union's my home and heart,
But my joys are with the Southland—
　　May its glories ne'er depart.

Glorious land, the Sunny Southland!
　　Meadows green and sparkling streams,
Beautiful land, perennial with flowers,
　　Fragrant as a fairy's dreams,
Thou wast the pride of my boyhood,
　　And fond mem'ry, brooding still,
A thousand pleasing fancies entwine
　　Round every rivulet and rill.

Thou land of sunshine and beauty,
　　Thou pride of manhood and youth,
Land of fair women and brave men,
　　Home of virtue and of truth,
May peace and plenty crown thee still
　　And freedom thy sons inspire,
While liberty draws in circles round
　　Its walls of flaming fire!

The harsh discord of grim battle
　　Has shaken thy sunny plains,
And the blood of thy bravest sons
　　A mother's warm bosom stains;
Crushed 'neath thy brothers' iron heels,
　　I've heard thy piteous groan,

I've seen thee deck the Northern graves
With flowers stripped from thy own.

Let victors parade their bloody shirts
And tell the world their story,
But lightly tread the Southern graves
They have digged for their glory.
Oh! mock us not, my dear friends,
If over these graves we weep,
Our souls are humble, our hearts are sore,
And our wounds are very deep.

We are trying to forget the past,
To bury its dead away,
To live for our country's glory,
Hopeful of a brighter day;
Let us wake no more the feelings,
Let the deep-mouthed cannons sleep
Where shadowy specters of battle
Their ghostly vigils keep.

God still smiles upon the Southland
Through the battle's gloomy spray,
The golden sun of prosperity
Is lighting up a better day;
Our hearts but warm with faith and hope,
The chains of slavery broken,
The spirit of love and liberty
Whispers a friendly token.

'TIS BUT A SIMPLE LOCK OF HAIR.

'Tis but a simple lock of hair,
'Tis but a faded curl,
And yet it has for me a charm,
The sweetest in the world;

Although she who gave it to me
　　Has long since passed away,
This little talisman is left
　　To compliment her memory.

Ah! well do I remember now
　　My heart's transcendent bliss,
She told me that she loved me true,
　　And sealed it with a kiss;
And then it was this raven lock
　　Was severed from the rest,
I vowed I'd wear it forever,
　　A charm upon my breast.

When she blushed so very sweetly,
　　To my bosom I held 't,
She was very young and modest
　　And begged me not to tell 't;
As I placed it in my bosom
　　I vowed it should ne'er part,
Death has taken away my love,
　　Death must tear 't from my heart.

We were but tiny children then,
　　When purest fancies rove,
But our pure thoughts were earnest
　　And our hearts were in love;
And though I have grown older, still,
　　In this world of wicked cares,
I never can forget the love
　　That thrilled my early years.

Why say it was a weak fancy
　　That broke my childish rest,
For though years have rolled between us
　　It lingers on my breast;

When I visit her little grave
    Where rests her slender form,
The same emotions come o'er me
    That used my heart to warm.

I sometimes meet her even now
    In the visions of night,
She moves a gentle, graceful form,
    Like an angel of light;
I mark her lovely, smiling face,
    Arched brow without its curl,
Then to my bosom press the lock—
    All's left me in the world.

THE 'PATHES.

There are allopaths and hydropaths,
    And homeopaths as brave,
But never a path 'mong all the paths
    But leads to the grave.

Some give thee infinitesimals,
    And some give larger pills,
But all of them are large enough
    When 't comes to the bills.

Some will vomit and some purge thee,
    Some dose the nerves for pains;
All deplete the patient's pockets,
    Though they will not his veins.

Some, Baptist-like, believe in water,
    Some 'lectrify each groan,
All have a credulous following
    And graveyards of their own.

Some claim to be true eclectics,
  Some's Indian doctors bawl;
There's little choice among the lot,
  They're Charon's agents all.

ANCIENT FAME.

What is fame to the silent dead,
  With its roll of classic years?
The marble shaft above the head
  Speaks indeed to living ears;
But death, long, eternal repose,
  Whether our friends laugh or weep,
Oblivious alike to joys and woes
  It's long, unbroken sleep.

Can a Cæsar or Alexander
  Hear again his hero name,
Tho' time's torturous course meanders
  Amid his undying fame?
Scattered by centuries of storms,
  Their crumbling dusts are strown,
And thro' a thousand changing forms,
  All senseless and unknown.

The sweet notes that blind Homer sung,
  Thrilled from heaven's choicest lyre,
Will linger on the human tongue
  Till all circling times expire;
This poet, who with throbbing brain
  Poesy's sweetest secrets broke,
Will hear no more the mellow strain
  His own fancy awoke.

Can Gautama and Mahomet,
    Tho' achieved their proud designs
With holy wisdom, even yet
    Hear suppliants at their shrines,
Where millions by blind faith
    Or fanatic creeds driven,
Seek the dark chambers of death,
    Dreaming that 't is heaven?

But such, alas! in truth, is fame,
    Enthusing ambitious men,
That they may die with swelling name,
    Engraved on the future ken—
Die like the beast, and rot and waste,
    Never, never hear again
Those deeds of glory or disgrace
    That make or unmake men.

I WISH I WAS A PREACHER.

Oh! I wish I was a preacher,
    Then it would be so sweet
To camp with the richest wethers
    And get good grub to eat;
But when the flock is impoverished
    It would n't suit so well,
I 'd leave the impecunious lambs
    To chance it for hell.

But where there are regal comforts,
    And where there 's princely grub,
I would sing the songs of Zion
    And float the gospel tub;
I know that salvation is free
    To all upon a level,

11

But the flock that is very poor
 Must shepherd with the devil.

I might find among the paupers
 Many God-fearing creatures,
But he's a pillar in the church
 Who helps to feed the preachers;
I'd look among the wealthy class
 For piety unmistaken,
I'd camp upon their downy beds
 And eat their eggs and bacon.

While I might serve my Lord and God
 By starving like a wizard,
Yet all the praise of ragged saints
 Can't ease a preacher's gizzard.
" You bet," I'd make the best of time,
 Whatever winds might waft'er;
There'll be little of the preaching cant
 In the great hereafter.

LOVE.

Youth for love, like flowers in spring time,
 And sweet its rose full blown,
Though autumn brings the fruit to prime,
 Its delicate tints are gone,
But comes no more exquisite youth
 When once its dreams have faded.
Sere winter's winds are chill and ruth,
 And autumn's streams 're shaded;
Or, if perchance winter's sun steals
 Thro' broken clouds unrolled,
Its smiles are shed o'er icy fields,
 As dreary as they're cold.

ENGLAND'S POETS LAUREATE.

O, come thou beast of Balaam's pride,
Come let the poets take a ride ;
We'll get the muses on astride,
    And then we'll sing
Such songs as Laureates provide
    To 'muse the king.

'T is sweet to hear the watch-dogs growl,
Guarding their master and his gold,
Rattle their chains, rant, and howl,
    The thieves to affright,
When only some ill-omened owl
    Hoots to the night.

So, poets of the crippled wing,
Tame falcons, to your masters cling,
There's bread in every song you sing
    For royal pleasure,
Ravished muses forth their verses bring
    In forced measure.

So, kenneled dogs, rattle your chains,
Proud of your collars and their stains,
When Freedom expires, o'er her remains
    Erect your thrones,
Laugh at the grief that swells her pains
    And mock her groans.

With affection's wicked guile
Go woo the tyrant's bloody smile,
And tell the people all the while
    It is Liberty
To enslave mankind and defile
    The brave and free.

Go flex your knees, ye pampered slaves,
Go carve your names on Freedom's graves!
Pollute Liberty, slander her braves,
    ·   And take the pelf
That tyrants wring from tortured slaves
        And feast yourself!

An aristocracy may be kind
To its slaves, but the slaves are blind,
When in a privileged class they find
        Such god-like things;
The halters round their necks they bind
        Who worship kings.

Mercenary 's the polluted lyre
Where Freedom hides its smoldering fire,
And forced the muses who inspire
        Its servile lays;
Dreading monarchy's bloody ire,
        They sing its praise.

O! tune thy harp, proud Liberty,
And sing of men, equal and free,
By heaven's and the earth's decree;
        No slaves nor kings,
Cursed be the bard, whoe'er he be,
        Bows to such things.

THE F. F. V'S.

We are the true sons of old Virginia,
  Come, common folks, get on your knees,
The blood in our veins is no common stuff,
  We are genuine F. F. V's.

Our dads killed Indians and danced the scalp-dance,
   And bought our dames with funked tobacco ;
No better blood flows thro' royalty's veins,
   Pray tell us then what we lack, sir. ·

Our great grandsires ruled this nation great,
   No people more honest or nicer ;
When Virginia cut the public cheese,
   We got the largest slice, sir.

But our negroes freed, our prestige gone,
   With glories of many a field,
The backbone of the South broken in twain,
   We're left only shabby genteel.

We'll remember the glory of days departed,
   And still bow our backs, like tom-cats,
Rub up the brass buttons on dad's old coats,
   And parade in his old cocked hats.

Our hearts as proud as our stomachs empty,
   From dad's moss grave hope plucks its rose ;
If we are not great, our sires were mighty,
   The children may wear their old clothes.

Posterity's ungenerous to the sons of the great;
   Where on its bottom must stand each tub,
Sons of the illustrious must toil and sweat
   Like other men's sons for their grub.

Oh! what a pity this great, great nation
   Has no empty titles to please
The pride of whim-inspired fools who dream
   There's glory in the F. F. V's.

THERE'S A GOOD OLD TIME A-COMING.

There's a good old time a-coming,
    Full of joy and full of praise,
And the swelling years are humming
    All the gladness of its days;
In my prophetic eye I trace
    Dissolving crowns and empires,
The visions of a nobler race
    My harp awakes and inspires.

There's a good old time a-coming,
    The right and wrong shall sever,
The cannon's murderous booming
    Be heard no more forever;
The kings and priests will till the soil,
    Treason nor heresy crimes,
Wealth grow only from honest toil,
    The harvest of good old times.

There's a good old time a-coming,
    When contentions all will cease,
War's grim foes no more consuming,
    All the nations dwell in peace;
Would that nature'd prolong my life   .
    To th' dawn of that better day,
When calumny's hushed, and th' tongue o' strife
    Is buried fore'er away.

There's a good old time a-coming,
    Make haste its glorious hours,
Darkness'll flee before its coming
    And vice shrink before its powers,
The sword and bayonet turn to rust—
    Hallelujah! our songs of glee,

Crowns and mitres trail in the dust,
  The people, the people are free!

There's a good old time a-coming,
  Reason will hold dominion,
None blessed for creed or cunning,
  None damned for mere opinion;
Reason, the torch-light of Liberty,
  Will illume life's dusky goals,
Nor kings nor priests enslave the free,
  Bind their hands or fetter their souls.

HOPE.

Hope is the lone star that guides the soul
  And lends to sorrow its beacon rays,
'Neath its beams the cares of life unroll
  In fleeting dreams of better days.

Howe'er dark the gloom of human grief,
  There are still some stars from out the night
That shine through broken clouds in dim relief
  And cheer up the weary soul with light.

The worn travellers 'long life's desert waste,
  With foot-steps sore pursue the dim light,
But the phantom recedes with equal haste
  And always remote though forever bright.

To weary invalid, racked with dire pain,
  'Tis counsel serene and heav'n inspiring,
It cools his thirst and soothes his aching brain,
  And cheers his soul even when dying.

Youth, inspired by deeds of glory profound,
  Kindles ambition at its burning flames,

And through mazy years yearns for the renown
   That fortune heaps on obscurest names.

And e'en age, tottering on the ragged brinks,
   Views with composure the ending strife,
Though from pleasure's streams no more it drinks,
   Its visions are of another life.

The fond maid who pins the rose on her breast,
   Blushing at the name she loves to hear,
Finds in her hopes a solace for unrest,
   And smiles as if the world had no tear.

The widowed heart, weighed down with fear and grief,
   Pining o'er the graves of loved ones lost,
And when all her bitter tears bring no relief,
   Hope illumes the wretch tho' tempest tossed.

To the Christian, tottering 'mid sin and death,
   'Gainst the powers of jealous hatred driven,
'Tis the calm softer than the lily's breath,
   The golden chain tethering life to heaven.

There is no night of human woe so dark,
   No anguish of human heart so deep,
That hope lends not the mind its beacon spark
   To light the dying soul to its sleep.

I AM NOT OLD, YET I HAVE SEEN.

I am not old, yet I have seen
In social ties sad faults I ween ;
Oh ! would to God I could erase
Some scenes that still disturb my peace.
If I was asked to manifest
The demons of the human breast,

The chiefs of life's unhallowed brood,
Are pride and base ingratitude!

I have seen the ungenerous son
With impious pride his father spurn,
Disown the germ that gave him name,
And shrink from his sire with shame,
As if the stream in its far course
Was purer than its fountain-source,
Or child could boast a social good
Superior to its father's blood;
Excepting not the real worth,
Nature's given the humblest birth,
Common stuff's the blood of kings
And all the caste who boast such things—
An honest man's as great as him
·Whose pride's a royal diadem.

And I have seen the father cast
His offspring from him like a beast,
And more inhuman than the brute,
Disown, dishonor, and refute,
As if the child in its worst stains
Was not the blood of its father's veins!
As well curse the child that's born blind
As t' curse it for its cast of mind;
However good, however rash,
The son is but the father's flesh.

But there is one friend, a mother,
With heart truer than all other:
Through the torturing throes of birth
She welcomes the little waif to earth,
The guardian of his tender years,
She soothes his pains and lulls his fears;

However high, however low,
Her prayers will follow whe'er he go;
When all others desert his weal,
Beside his dying couch she'll kneel,
And in the face of black despair
With yearning heart pour out her prayer,
Whether dying with glory blessed
Or a culprit at the law's behest;
There is no crime so black, so deep,
O'er which a mother may not weep.

Why then repeat the slander vile,
Woman herself is sin's own child,
That in some dark, mysterious way
Angelic man she led astray,
Companioned with a demon base
To ruin herself and damn the race,
Her tiny arm broke Eden's spell,
Unbarred the iron gates of hell.
Rather unbosom society's wound,
'Tis wicked man has dragged her down
And tried to shield his infernal deed
With legends of a holy creed,
As if the slander would be sweet
That heaven's libeled to repeat.
Confiding in her purer trust,
A creature of man's baser lust,
She yields whatever gives her pain,
He turns and slanders her again.

Woman, thine is the nobler part,
Thine the true instincts of the heart;
Seraphic form to angels akin,
Tempted by man alone to sin,
Though all the demons out of hell

And all angels unite to swell
A wicked story, vile and base,
I 'll ne'er believe in thy disgrace.
Rather say, from depths of sin,
Where not a ray of light broke in,
As black as hell, as dark as night,
Woman smiled the dawning light,
Dispelled the clouds of moral gloom
That wrapped the world's unhallowed tomb.

Man, wouldst thou thy legends retain,
Revise thy holy book again,
Have thyself, where Eden's nectar drips,
Pressing sin to woman's pure lips!

THE CENTURY PARTY.

Our girls were out the other day,
  Costumed strange and antique,
Their manners queer and ancient styles
  Of by-gone days did speak;
As we gazed upon the happy throng
  We thought of some no more,
Who graced such styles with charming smiles
  A hundred years ago.

We looked upon the sweetest faces,
  'Neath hats so quaint and old;
No wonder, woman 's lovely still,
  Be the fashion ne'er so droll!
No wonder our grandsires loved the dames,
  Wooed them with tenderest care!
Their pretty faces had charming graces
  Despite the powdered hair.

The big sun-bonnet, all o'er the head,
   Hid many a charm away,
Their hearts as true and cheeks as red
   As any are now-a-day,
Their blushes as sweet, their eyes as bright,
   Their waists as neat and slender—
But one thing I mind, our granddames behind,
   That's the Grecian bender.

When a hundred years shall pass us by,
   Sweet girls will comique our time,
And the world laugh at our fashions queer,
   Though we think they're sublime;
But woman'll have a cheering smile,
   Her form angelic and petite,
Howe'er you dress her, man'll e'er caress her,
   And swear the fashion's sweet.

THE DISSECTING-ROOM, CHRISTMAS NIGHT, 1872.

The dim lamps are lighted,
   The victims are unspread,
The phantom shadows creep
   O'er the grim-visaged dead;
Half a hundred human forms,
   Now but the wrecks of life,
Unshrouded and ghastly,
   Await the student's knife.

They're here whose friends to-night,
   Merry with wine and song,
Little dream of science's right
   Or of society's wrong.

Death makes them equal here,
  The ruthless knife of fate
Will ne'er inquire their names,
  Their titles or estate.

We gaze upon shrunken forms,
  Filled with sad misgiving,
Though the world is gay enough
  Mingling with the living,
In the presence of death
  Gayeties all confound us—
Shadowy forms from spirit-land
  Are hovering round us.

The world is merry to-night
  And man on pleasure bent,
E'en now the blood-hounds o' Death
  Are hot upon his scent;
Death's abroad with glass and scythe,
  But man still undismayed,
Frenzied from pleasure's cup,
  Meets the unerring blade.

Here from palace and hovel,
  God only knows each name,
And ruthless knife of science
  Is ignorant o' the same;
O'er this human butchery,
  O'er this carnage and gore,
Students smile like savants,
  All proud of savage lore.

Many graves by flowers wreathed
  The truth will ne'er disclose,
Th' sculptured pride's a mockery
  That speaks of sweet repose;

Friends'll gather round the grave
　To speak of worth and faults,
Where stately shafts lift their forms
　'Bove the empty vaults.

Would you know life's vanities,
　Its pleasures bought so dear,
Look at the world's greedy strife
　Ignobly ending here;
The soft whisperings of flattery
　Are senseless to these ears,
Glory may fill life with pride,
　Death neither smiles nor tears.

Could these cold forms but speak,
　What would they say to-night
Of all they've left behind,
　Of happy homes and bright?
Some struggled hard with death,
　Clung to life so fondly,
As if earth was all hope
　And death blank eternity;

Some, frenzied with weird grief,
　Insane visions inspire,
Fevered blood tortured the brain
　With forms grotesque and dire;
Some, serene as fading day
　Shadowing evening's light,
As calmly bade them adieu,
　Welcoming its long night;

Some had fancies, hopeful, bright,
　To flit before the brain,
Some, convulsed in horrid fright,
　Battled with fiends in flame;
Some fond souls, who ne'er dreamed
　Life's frail tenure so short,

Passed through unconscious sleep
  To death without a thought.

We'll pile their bones together,
  All in one common heap,
Where we've laid the flesh away,
  A thousand bodies sleep;
Men, women, and children, all
  In one foul pit distressed,
Moldering slowly back to earth—
  God grant their spirits rest.

Perhaps the souls of the dead
  Stand guard around these walls,
And though we hear not their tread,
  March silent through its halls;
Or, why this fearful silence
  That fills the heart with dread,
And why this strange oppression
  While standing by the dead?

Who knows but this very night,
  While the world's on a spree,
Here in this Dissecting-room
  They hold their jubilee;
The spirits may be content,
  More than our hopes can tell,
Unprisoned from their bodies
  As from a useless shell.

And ne'er a soul gathered here
  Will pine away for grief,
Knowing its body is lent
  All for human relief.
Oh! what ghost would not proudly,
  That science might not starve,
Bequeath its body gladly
  For young saw-bones to carve?

OUR CREEDLESS GOD AND HIS CREATURE, MAN.

Whether influenced for good or ill,
Man's creation's enigma still,
Lord of all, in reason sublime,
He rules supreme in every clime;
A god in all pride can impute,
In passion lower than the brute,
Hate, love, fear, hope, all, all profound,
Whate'er makes man or drags him down,
That brings honor or brings disgrace,
Is the heritage of his race.
  As here I sit in pensive mood,
O'er the past my fancies brood,
And from creation's cosmic birth
I trace the flight of time and earth;
Where'er I mark creation's plan,
The central figure is always man.
Through the dreary chaotic waste,
Through the cycles of ages past,
Ere from out eternal quiet
Light first sprang at nature's fiat,
Ere from the tumult of the deep
Life awoke from organic sleep,
Nature ruled; immutable laws
Guided the sun, moon, and the stars.
  But how came he—where, whence, when,
The presumptive creature called man?
The structures of his life proclaim
He's but a link in nature's chain,
Every fiber of his being
In strong accord and agreeing;

But whence his source, majestic plan,
The cause is God, the effect, man ;
And this as deep as we can look,
Despite of sage or holy book.

Like other beast his way man plods ;
As if twin brother to the gods
He scorns the menial tribes of earth,
Denies his own terrestial birth,
With pride high's the sky, deep's the sea,
Boasts a celestial pedigree.

Ah! mortal man, is it not pride
Separates thee from all beside,
Bequeathing human flesh and blood
An immortality of good,
Leaving other organic life
To waste itself in brutal strife?
Is it not egotism bold
That gives to thee alone a soul
To ride 'bove empyrean fires
When ev'ry other life expires?
Is it not thy insatiate pride
That builds its heaven broad and wide,
And thy jealous hate that extends
A hell for all except thy friends?

Behold the Indian in his wild,
Far from the home of Christian guile,
Buries his friend with dog and knife
To attend him in his spirit life!
And four times when the night returns,
O'er his grave a fire burns
To light his manes beyond this bound
To a happier hunting-ground ;
Nor Christian priest nor learned divine
Swerves him from customs of time,

From sacred legends handed down,
Traditioned from ancient renown.
    See the Moslem, whom Christians spurn,
His dying eyes toward Mecca turn,
With expiring breath speak a weal
That makes the shuddering skeptic reel;
Behold, with what undying grace
Faith mocks grim death e'en to his face!
    Hear the Brahmin's exulting shout
When great Juggernaut is brought out,
Where pious friends with prayerful breath
Implore the maimed to seek for death,
Beneath the wheels to crush their cares
And be transformed in other spheres.
    Behold mankind of every faith
Rejoice in woe, exult in death!
From fiery stakes and dungeon cells
Strengthen the creed, warn infidels;
To that fond egotism given
That elects self the choice of heaven,
And builds a spacious mansion grand
For special grace ere time began.
Turn, if you will, to Christian lands,
Behold the thief with gory hands!
In his vile history you may trace
A thousand crimes of black disgrace,
Too infamous for pen to tell,
Dark as night, as filthy as hell.
When justice can no more endure,
The thief's conscience, light and pure,
Turns upward from his crimes in prayer
And faces death without a fear;
Saved by grace and not by deeds,
Saved by faith in Christian creeds.

Honest heathens, in whose dark night
Has never shone the gospel light,
If saved at all, with broken string
A rusty harp to heaven bring,
Morality must take its seat
And wash the faithful murderer's feet.
Saved! oh, no, too foul their crimes,
However righteous in their times;
Though pure in life, the wrong in faith
Must be damned to eternal death.

Behold the land where faiths extend,
And cross and crescent closely blend!
Behold, side by side are lying
The Moslem and Christian, dying!
A rival god, a rival faith,
Exults each in triumphant death;
Blessed lights, divinely shed,
Cheer the living and save the dead.
Islam's daughter, dying, blesses
The prophet, to her bosom presses
The Koran; rejoicing the light
Is hers, tho' the rest are in night.
Christian daughter, dying, blesses
The Gospel, to her bosom presses
Its hopes; rejoicing it's given
To lead the faithful to heaven.

Men see pure mercy manifest
That saves the few and damns the rest,
Provided only this grace undue
Makes them partakers with the few.
What are human creeds but mere breath,
Mythical creatures of our faith!
What's faith in all its relations,
The color of our educations!

Bosoms, inspired, blaze when fanned
By legends from the Father-land;
Traditions saved from ancient night
Serve the people for sacred light,
By subtle priest allured or frightened,
The slaves believe and are enlightened.
Where once a faith gains current force,
The powers of hell can't turn its course;
The maddening stream rushes wildly on,
And deep and wide the channel's torn.

'S well tempt to shake the mountain base
As stop the growth of Mormon grace;
The priests but howl their dismal tales,
The people hear in frightful wails;
Whatever truths by faith possessed,
They're ne'er to the masses addressed;
Superstition finds ready soil
Where childhood plays with artless guile,
It grows with manhood's growth apace
Till 't poisons all the human race.

However different be the creeds,
Whether Mahomet fights or Jesus bleeds,
Each nation with egotism crams,
Itself elects, all others damns,
Arrogating to its favored race,
Immortality of love and grace.

Why should faith be only merit
We from our fathers inherit,
Whether our glory or our shame,
We've our fathers' God all the same?
Tho' ev'ry word of innovation
Shocks the pride of the nation,
Ev'ry word of pure reason
Classed by state and clergy treason.

But if the rule's to us applied,
Oh! why to other lands denied,
Where old legends have witness borne
Miracles greater than our own?

Man, poor creature of the sod,
Adoring a proscriptive God,
With selfishness sadly blessed,
Saves himself to damn the rest.

Give me a man with heart and soul
Broad as the universal whole!
Give me a God creedless and free
As the heart of a man should be!
Great Power Supreme, who rules the land
And shapes the destinies of man,
'Tis priestcraft that would circumscribe
Thy tender love to race or tribe;
Where'er extends the human race
Spreads Thy benediction of grace,
Free as the sunlight and the dews
Thy tenderest mercies diffuse;
In ev'ry age, whate'er Thy name,
To all mankind, one God, the same.

PREDESTINATION.

Thou whom God alone respected,
By eternal grace selected,
Where all others are rejected
    As vile and gory,
Predestined, called and elected
    All for His glory.

O! thou who art a chosen race,
Tune now thy harps to partial grace;

Sing of joys that ne'er will cease
    Beyond the sky,
Of hope, of love, eternal peace,
    Ne'er more to die.

Look toward yon radiant strand,
Far beyond time's fleeting sand,
Behold a bright angelic band,
    All saved by grace;
Sweet notes swelling the heav'nly land—
    Serene our peace.

Music sweet to heaven-born ears,
It lulls to sleep their saintly fears;
Haloes of glory round their cares
    Stream from above,
Thousands bask in the smiling spheres
    Of elected love.

Look down into the abyss of hell,
Where fiery waves recede and swell;
Oh! hear the damned roar and yell
    Where hope despairs,
Then in the strains of mercy tell
    What grace is theirs.

Eternal night of hopeless despair,
No sun, no moon, no friendly star
To light its gloom or soothe its care—
    Elected to hell;
Remorseless conscience with weird glare
    Broods o'er the cell.

Not of merit but 'lected grace,
The few who see God's smiling face;
Unborn, they were a chosen race,
    Refined treasure,

Brands torn from burning disgrace
For heav'n's pleasure.

Before creation's sublime morn
Eternal conceptions took form,
Order sprang from chaos and storm ;
   Our woes began,
And vaulted hell was heated warm
   To torture man.

Backward roll time's circling flight
Into the dusky shades of night,
Ere God had said " Let there be light,"
   And it was given,
Souls yet unborn, in mystic night
   Purposed for heaven.

Still the elect, shouting, proclaim
Grace alone is redemption's scheme,
And justify a hell of shame—
   Predestined sorrows,
Where others must reap all the bane
   Of its horrors.

Why's our God so very partial,
In love mild, in vengeance martial,
Serene in heaven, fierce in hell,
   To helpless creature?
Sure all this inspiration fell
   Upon the preacher.

God ne'er gave a reluctant smile
To a wayward and sin-born child
To please the craft, the priestly guild,
   That always delves
To control his patronizing smile
   All to themselves.

Ere to such depths of woe we sink,
Let's pause on eternity's brink
And think of God, as one would think
　　Who never dreams;
But every thirsty soul may drink
　　At mercy's streams.

As we know not the hearts of men,
Judge them lightly, lest we offend
Some virtuous conscience whose end
　　Is peace profound,
Tho' black clouds to mortal ken
　　Gather around.

O! my soul weary not with grief
But look to heaven for relief,
E'en on the cross the dying thief
　　May hear the call;
God binds the world in his great sheaf,
　　Mercy weeps for all.

ANSWER TO A YOUNG LADY'S REQUEST NOT TO TELL.

Young lovers, when riding out,
　　Should not be cloyed with bliss,
But keep their wits about them
　　And look before they kiss;
I don't deny the pleasure
　　Is not for every one,
The presence of a stranger,
　　You know, may spoil the fun.

I 'd have hid my eyes, sweet lass,
   But how was I to know
That I was uninvited
   Until I saw the show?
I 'll not connive at evil,
   For folly I 've no price,
But the touch of innocent lips
   Is sacred as 't is nice.

I 'm a connoisseur of good things,
   A sweet kiss I know it,
As perfume to the flower is,
   So love is to the poet;
True love is unsuspecting,
   Of confidence 't is born,
When you pluck its rose, my dear,
   Oh do n't forget its thorn.

OUR COUNTRY.

Land of Liberty and civil pride,
   No crowned tyrants mar thy rest,
No mitred despots e'er preside
   To nurse the vigor from thy breast;
Fair and free by nature designed,
   Liberal in all that is good
And elevating to the mind;
   Freedom crushed every unhallow'd brood,
   And sealed thy sacred rights with its blood.

What galling chains have been broken
   By men, who gave their lives and all,
That Liberty might be outspoken,
   Freedom bequeathed to one and all;

. The grandest men who have tasted
　　Of tyranny's cup bitter as gall,
On fields of blood their lives wasted,
　　That we might survive the call
　　And reap the glorious harvest of their fall.

'T is not in vain the patriot dies,
　　When around his most sacred grave
Grateful people with tear-dimmed eyes
　　Spread flowers o'er the martyred brave ;
'T is not in vain the patriot dies,
　　When Freedom's sons, no longer slaves,
Exalt his memory to the skies,
　　Who broke their chains, unbarred their caves,
　　And flung Liberty's ensign where it waves.

Ye who fear neither priest nor kings
　　Nor inquisitions all gory,
Know thou the price Liberty brings
　　As a ransom for your glory,
How noble men on battle field,
　　Our country's sires, sage and hoary,
Preferred to die rather than yield ?
　　On your hearts engrave the story,
　　To you they 've bequeathed undying glory.

" Eternal vigil 's the price of liberty,"
　　Then guard well your sacred treasure,
Be ever ready, sons of the free,
　　Your swords with tyrants to measure ;
Oh ! guard well each time-embalmed right
　　From church and lordly pleasure,
And be the day-star ever bright
　　That leads the brave man to measure
　　Human rights above all human treasure.

THE UNION.

May the States survive forever,
  Peopled numerous as the sand,
Liberty open wide its arms
  To the slaves of ev'ry land.
Oh! may I live to see the day
  The world shall read our story,
When a hundred stately stars
  Spangle America's glory.

When from the winding Rio Grande
  To Canada's frozen zone
All the altars of the nation
  Are one common hearth-stone;
When the jealousies of sections
  Are forgotten with the slain,
And sweetest flowers softly bloom
  On each bloody battle plain;

When intelligence and progress
  In holy union conspire
To bear aloft the great ensign
  Of Freedom and Empire.
Though native of Old Kentuck,
  Of the dark and bloody ground,
My heart is with the Union,
  Extensive as its bound.

He who truly loves his country
  Makes ev'ry State his home,
Loves no more its present greatness
  Than its grandeur to come.
God grant, although my eyes shall close,
  The Union will never cease;
Oh! may I last see my country
  In its glory and peace.

OLD AGE IN LOVE.

The tenderest passions of true love
 That enthuse the heart of youth,
And vibrate in softest accords,
 Shatter age with pitiless ruth,
Wild with weird discords.

The dreams that young lovers dream,
 In confiding arms entwined,
No thrilling emotions impart,
 Aged love is decrepit and blind,
Withered, and cold in heart.

Then fairest maids trust not thy charms
 To the arms of frigid age,
Tempted by grandeur's sordid gold ;
 As well the daisy by thy prestige
Bloom on a glacier cold.

Too soon the withering blast 'll come,
 So Time and Nature's decreed ;
'Tis written on each solemn page,
 No cold memory on love can feed
Or warm the heart of age.

Trust not the charms of youth to age ;
 Let passions kindle mutual fires,
And congenial tempers e'er move
 The blazing streams of youthful desires ;
Age can only chill love.

ADDRESS TO THE DEVIL, JULY 4, 1880.

O! thou who in yon cavern grim,
  Where infernal fire eternally rolls,
Who sits upon damnation's brim
  To scorch poor, unregenerate souls,
Art thou lonely in thy gloomy den
  Or tortured by fiendish desire?
Thou 'st naught to do but roast poor men,
  Allured to fuel thy fire.

In many pictures men portray thee—
  Horned, hoofed, and with cloven tongue,
With long barbed tail to dismay the
  ˙Faint-hearted, both old and young;
Some have thee a roaring lion,
  Crouching fiercely for thy prey,
Then, like the soft music of Zion,
  Leading even the saints astray.

Once we are told, an angel bright,
  All was serene and heaven smiled,
Ere down beneath the shades of night,
  By dire sin thou wast exiled.
O! tell us, for we long to know
  The origin of this fiery din ;
Thou tempted mankind to his woe,
  Who tempted thee to sin?

How long has this sad feud lasted,
  Where the good and bad contend?
How many ages have been wasted,
  Will it never find an end?
If God contends for the right
  And thou adverse, Sir Devil,

Why does not the stronger might
  Crush out the weaker evil?

Some have thee eternal, uncreated,
  Tho' forever steeped in sin,
Jealous of God till at last defeated,
  Hell was digged to chain thee in.
Is it still to revenge this mandate,
  Exiling thee from heaven's band,
That wreaking with unvenomed hate
  Thou 'd ensnare the creature, man?

Who loosed the iron chains of hell,
  Who burst wide its brazen-bars,
That thou might climb from gloomy cell
  To earth through clouds and stars?
Was it by Jehovah's permission,
  Or by thy own subtle power,
Thyself in serpent-shape did fashion
  To carry death in Eden's bower?

If naught but thy wicked jealousy
  Conspired the ruin of man,
O, where was the omniscient eye,
  Where the omnipotent hand?
Saw God not in thy sneaking form
  The woes of unborn nations,
As thou stole with murderous pride 'mong
  The fairest of his creations.

Is 't not enough that by the fall
  Man 's doomed to mortal misery?
Why still with venom's bitter gall
  Pursue his wretched progeny?
Why dig a pit deep in the night,
  Pave its access with fond desire,

Alluring with phantom delight
    Souls to a deceitful fire?

Why strew the path with scented flowers
    That leads mankind down to hell,
Why drive him 'long through lovely bowers,
    Through landscape fair and pleasant dell?
Why place him here on probation,
    His predestined woes to swell,
If long enough before creation
    His doom was sealed in hell?

One alternate all must admit
    Who believe in Adam's fall,
Thou art here by God's own permit,
    Or thou art not here at all;
Thou art a part of heaven's desire,
    A part of heaven's own plan;
As God directs, so flames thy fire,
    God's permit is God's command.

Then, Old Nick, Satan, or Devil,
    Have mercy on us common folks,
If thou art truly the prince of evil
    And not the butt of priestly jokes.
We own great power in skeptic incline,
    O, forgive us if we doubt thee;
To save our souls, we can't divine ·
    How the church could do without thee.

If burning people be thy trade,
    Why is it so appalling!
What man among us, tried and staid,
    But prides him in his calling!
Then fare thee well, old Nickie, friend,
    However vile ye 're tainted,
I 'll neither slander nor defend
    Till we are better 'quainted.

YOU ASK ME FOR A SONG, BOYS.

You ask me for a song, boys,
 To commemorate the slain
Who fell in our civil war
 On every hill and plain;
And I am born a Southron,
 Proud of the birth and name,
How can I sing the cause lost
 To all but bloody fame?

I dearly love my country,
 I hate a cause 't would sever
The union of Freedom's States,
 Linked by God forever.
How can I sing of chivalry,
 Of grim war's fierce display,
Where brother butchered brother
 And father son did slay?

Moldering in the quiet earth,
 We've laid them long away,
Their spirits to the God of battle,
 Their bodies to decay.
They were never foreign foes,
 But brothers and warm friends—
All children of sister States,
 Where kinship nearly blends.

Oh! sweet may their restings be,
 The sons of the blue and gray,
Now their spirits contend no more
 In the great eternity;
From the bloody field of battle,
 From its carnage and its strife,
They may strike an armistice
 'Neath the spreading Tree of Life.

I might sing of heroisms
Deserving a golden wreath,
Brave men to the cannon's mouth
Charged in the face of death;
I might sing of gallantry
'Mid battle's fiercest array,
But it pains my heart to count the dead
Whether of the blue or gray.

How can I sing of my country,
Gory with crimsoned strife?
How can I praise the valor
That seeks a brother's life?
When I visit their quiet grave,
'T is tears of remorse and shame;
O God, protect my country
From civil war again!

O God, inspire the patriot
In Freedom's honest toils,
And thwart the base demagogue
Who lives for party spoils!
May men of brain and moral worth,
With hearts as true and warm,
Stand bravely at the helm of state
And clear the rocks and storm.

THE MANIAC.

Is it madness,
This strange sadness,
    That forecasts its bitter goal?
Tell me truly,
Quickly, surely,

What power unruly
　Fetters my groaning soul.

Wild eyes beaming,
Fiercely streaming,
　In fiendish derision ;
Am I dreaming?
Is this seeming
Fiery gleaming
　But a frenzied vision ?

Souls undaunted,
Spirits haunted,
　Condemned to torturing shame,
Forever smiling,
My soul defiling,
My blood boiling
　In an infernal flame.

Yes, 't is madness,
This strange sadness,
　It forecasts its bitter goal ;
In my mad brain
Fierce demons reign,
And mock the pain
　That crazes my weird soul.

Grim-visaged Death
With fiery breath
　Tortures my burning soul ;
This iron cell
Is a grated hell—
Here fierce fiends dwell
　And chorus ev'ry howl.

Infernal desire,
Like balls o' fire,
　Rolls through every vein ;

The devils rend me,
My God, defend me,
Let death end me
    Of these infernal pains!

My clinking chains
Revive the pains,
    And tell my tale o' sadness;
Strange confusions,
Spectral intrusions,
Fiery delusions—
    Surely this is madness!

KENTUCKY.

Kentucky, my native home,
    I love thy name and fates,
I love thy mountains and vales,
    Proud sister of the States!
O, may thou ever cherish
    For Liberty a smile!
Oh, may they quickly perish,
    Who would thy sons beguile!

Thou once dark and bloody ground,
    Now peaceful smiles adorn,
Bright and fair thy pleasant homes
    And fields of waving corn;
No longer the fierce battle
    With blood thy forest stains,
Where gentle herds of cattle
    Feed on thy grassy plains.

I love thee, O land of my pride,
    By heaven richly blessed,

Great statesmen and great warriors
　Have been cradled on thy breast;
I love thy forests and hills,
　Thy thousand winding streams,
Thy gushing fountains and rills,
　Sparkling like fairy dreams.

No State in all the Union
　Can boast itself thy peer,
Thou home of modest virtue,
　Brave men and women fair.
I love thy cities, each temple,
　Thy halls of wealth and state,
Thy scenery, broad and ample,
　With nature profligate.

I boast for thee no foolish pride,
　No aristocratic birth,
But a State of loyal Freemen,
　With hearts of honest worth;
I love the Union dearly,
　I love each sister State,
Where lives and hearts and treasures
　Are linked in common fate.

My pride is in the Union
　And the glory that awaits,
When a hundred stars'll spangle
　The ensign of the States,
When from mountain-top and valley
　The voice of Freedom's hurl'd—
Land of fraternal union,
　The glory of the world.

Should bloody tyrants aspire
　To build on thy ruin their thrones,

Heaven some humble bard inspire
With Freedom's dying groans;
Let him thrill the sacred lyre
In the ears of menial slaves,
While Liberty's smould'ring fire
Yet burns upon our graves.

We'll hear the minstrel's sad strains
Echoing through dusky caves,
'T will wake the spirits of our dead
From out their deepest graves;
The proud spirits of our Fathers
Will marshal on every plain,
Where'er the sons of Liberty
Fight Freedom's battles again.

SPRING.

Oh, how happy the joyous Spring!
The earth's filled with its merry ring,
From ev'ry grove, from ev'ry tree,
The little warblers sing sweetly;
How softly glide the passing hours,
Perfumed with a thousand flowers,
Bright as fancy's radiant dream
Is nature clothed in gold and green!

Winter awakes from his sleep
Like some monster from the deep,
Shakes his frozen locks, and then
Smiles upon the world again;
From frosted breath the clouds diffuse
And melt into the gentler dews,
So breaks the chain of Nature's slave
And looses Spring from Winter's grave.

The fountains gushing from the hills,
Rippling glide in sparkling rills,
No longer bound by Winter's chains,
They gently flow through grassy plains;
The little birds with merry song
Greet them as they pass along,
Timid flowers on every side
In lovely array nod to the tide.

Then from ice-fields darkly sleeping
The verdant grass comes gently creeping,
Lovely flowers softly springing,
Every grove and field is ringing;
All nature thrills itself with song,
A thousand voices still prolong,
Harmonies vie in gentle strife,
The world is full of joy and life.

Of all seasons, the Spring I love,
None other that has charms to move
The heart and soul on fancy's wing
Like gentle, love-inspiring Spring;
The season when young lovers stray
Where flowers fill the gladsome way,
And sceneries fresh combined impart
Their kindred joys to the heart.

I have often thought of the time
I should quit this frame of mine,
I've wondered on the strange powers
That might charm its dusky hours;
And though no light has ever strayed
Into this cloudy realm of shade,
Let me die 'mid Spring's bright shining,
Soft as the light from day declining.

THE RURAL DOCTOR.

A gay old lark's the rural Doctor,
　A regular country swell;
The village pill and joke concoctor
　Every body wishes well.

It minds him not how dark or dreary,
　He is always on the go,
He never seems to tire or weary,
　Nor stop for rain or snow.

It's midnight, a storm is blowing,
　Lightnings flash, thunders roar,
Still he must be up and going—
　There's a caller at his door.

Up the mountains, over the hills,
　Despite the wind and the rain,
Onward he dashes, rattling pills,
　Hunting human gripes and pains.

But the Doctor's a jovial fellow,
　Full of pranks, heedless of care;
An inveterate old story-teller,
　He is welcome ev'ry where.

The village counsel and adviser,
　Ev'ry body's secret-keeper;
None are truer, none are wiser,
　None of truth had drunk deeper.

He's at ev'ry birth, ev'ry marriage,
　Be the weather foul or fair;
Ev'ry thing would bring miscarriage,
　If the Doctor was not there.

Rural doctors 're getting scarcer,
　City styles are now employed,

The race for wealth's maddening faster,
  Charity is all destroyed,
The dear old family Doctor passes
  Back into another age,
Baldhead specialists with eye-glasses
  Are becoming all the rage.

ONE GOD, THE SAME.

God of nature, broad and wide,
  In universal fame,
To whate'er myth faith's applied,
  Thou art worshiped all the same;
Allah, Jehovah, Brahma, Jove,
  Men bow before thy shrine,
Round thy temples faith and love
  In sacred memories twine.

Thy name's emblazed on ev'ry star,
  Written on ev'ry flower,
The sons of Gautama see it there
  In its majestic power;
It flashes in the lightning's glare,
  Roars in the thunders warm,
The pagan hears and breathes his prayer
  To the maddening storm.

'Mid forest deep and dark as night,
  Around his wigwam fires,
The Indian sees Thee shining bright
  As his bosom inspires.
Who art Thou, great power to move
  All men, both great and small,
Allah, Jehovah, Brahma, Jove,
  Either of these, or all?

Of the whisp'rings from cloudy spheres,
  Celestial visions fired,
Breathed by priest in mortal ears,
  Which of all is inspired;
Bible, Koran, or Vedas hoary,
  Which of these are shamm'd?
All'd have us believe their story
  Or be forever damned.

Where'er extends terrestrial sod
  Or lives Thy faithful creatures,
Thy glories, O, Eternal God!
  Are money to the preachers;
The footmen of crescent or cross
  Must meet the battle's clash,
Shed all the blood's shed for the cause—
  The priests get all the cash.

The pallid face of ghastly death,
  The memories of the tomb,
A gloomy hell yawning beneath
  Gives every creed a boom;
The sinner must be frightened
  With the Devil's demerit,
The elect all better enlightened
  By torturing the spirit.

Let us reason on the nations
  Where the gods are not brothers,
Priests of rival inspirations
  Malign and damn all others;
Let the Christian curse old Islam,
  And Islam return the blow,
God will bless the liberal men
  When fanatics are no more.

DYING FEARS.

Why speak to me of dying fears,
 Groans of sad misgiving,
When saw ye in the coffin tears
 Unwept by the living?

A thief may die with smiling face,
 Good men die repining;
The evidence of death for 'grace
 Is irrelevant finding.

Disease may craze the purest mind,
 Subvert ev'ry emotion,
Till saints blaspheme like demons blind
 Or base melt in devotion.

The great, the low, all, all must die,
 Death is unrelenting,
Hears neither saint or sinner cry,
 Mocking or repenting.

When I go by Nature's decree,
 Victim to mortal pains,
Let no ranting priest howl o'er me
 Nor slander my remains.

Let not my cold dissolving form,
 As senseless as the clay,
Be used to frighten bosoms warm
 Nor timid hearts dismay.

THE DEVIL'S DEAD.

Courage, friends, the Devil's dead,
　His reign of terror's o'er,
Round his infernal altar spread,
By a crafty priesthood shed,
　Are lakes of human gore.

'Mid Inquisition's kindling fires
　He ruled with power divine,
Superstition thro' mighty empires
Counseled his infernal desires
　And bowed before his shrine.

Thro' carnage, thro' dungeons and fire,
　You may track his bloody ways;
Hid as from a pestilence dire
Or wailing 'neath infernal ire,
　Truth hied from mortal gaze.

Reason, champion of human right,
　First bid his powers defiance,
And thro' the dusky halls of night
Pursued the demon, gleaming bright
　The sword of Truth and Science.

Courage, friends, the Devil's dead,
　His iron chains are broken,
The wretched priests who earn their bread
Dealing in fire and melted lead
　His requiem have spoken.

I SOMETIMES REMEMBER.

I sometimes remember
  The days that are passed,
From their dying embers
  The future is forecast ;
Youth had many treasures,
  And, though I'm growing old,
To recall its pleasures
  Still warms my soul.

Fair childhood's fancies bright,
  Its thousand fairy dreams,
Like the fading twilight
  Wane in gentle beams ;
How I love to restore,
  As memory is fraught,
The days that come no more
  Save in musing thought.

Oh ! how like the dreaming
  Some pleasing vision o'er,
Bright hours are beaming
  From lovely days of yore ;
But life's fondest treasures
  The shears of Time 'll sever,
Childhood's fleeting pleasures
  Return no more forever.

Still I'm growing older
  In this land of decay,
The frigid world's colder
  As the years pass away ;
Youth, with buoyant gladness,
  Is deepening into gloom,

Age, with dusky sadness,
　Is shadowing the tomb.

This feasting on pleasures
　That have flown for aye,
Like counting lost treasures
　To wretched poverty ;
But why need we sorrow
　O'er days forever gone,
Has this life no morrow
　With its bright smiling morn ?

Though shadows from the grave
　Around us are stealing
True hearts, once young and brave,
　Are ne'er dead to feeling;
A brighter hope is dawning
　In its refulgence bright,
Silver beams of morning
　Gild the fading night.

THE SUICIDE.

The gaunt wolf is howling
　Around my humble shed,
My shivering wife and child
　Are crying for bread ;
Affliction's ruthless hands
　Lash me to my bed.

Winter's blasts are rattling
　Beneath my creaking door,
The cold winds are streaming
　Through cracks in the floor ;

No food's been provided,
   And I am sick and poor.

The world is cold and selfish,
   It passes heedless by,
Unheard's affliction's groans
   And poverty's wretched cry;
E'en death's unrelenting,
   Tho' I have prayed to die.

Death's marked me for its own,
   But lingers in the strife;
Oh! why should I prolong
   The remnant of a life,
Where nature but struggles
   To mock a starving wife!

No, I will end this life
   That has only its bane,
Relieve cold charity,
   And myself of pain;
Let the world say "He's mad,
   Fever frenzied his brain!"

I know they will wonder
   The rashness of the deed,
Who ne'er knew the sorrow
   That makes my heart to bleed,
Who ne'er felt affliction's hands,
   Nor poverty's wretched need.

'T is weak sentimentalism
   That bids me not to go,
My sentence has been given,
   But death respites the blow
Till fiends, torturing me,
   Add cruelty to woe.

Whether to dark oblivion
  Or in the jaws of hell
My poor soul is sinking,
  No power can break the spell;
This mad infatuation
  Is tolling its own knell.

But I hope for a rest
  This world has ne'er given,
And I pray to my God
  This deed may be forgiven,
May I yet find repose
  Eternally in heaven.

Let us plant a wild thorn
  Over his lonely grave,
Emblem of the sorrow
  His weary life did pave,
And the anguish of soul
  That bound him like a slave.

SECTARIANISM.

Is the great God divided
  'Mongst a thousand schisms,
Each denomination claiming
  The orthodox isms;
One Lord, one Faith, one Baptism,
  One Church supremely blessed,
Where God smiles serenely
  But frowns on all the rest?
As we gaze on the confusion
  That clouds this rival might,

We pity the great Divinity
  In such a curious plight.

The Catholics with crafty priest—
  Though recking with pollution,
Fifteen cents pays for mass
  And gives you absolution ;
While some go to heaven straight,
  Some via purgatory,
A teaspoonful of holy grease
  Will slide you into glory ;
This big church with its little god
  Still might rule the nations,
Had not matrimony and Luther
  Started the Reformations.

The Presbyterians, with stockings blue,
  To rich blood related,
Were predestined to heaven
  Before they were created ;
Their faces long and sour
  With Puritanic guile,
They expect to get to glory
  Because they never smile ;
They boast a sure election,
  This theocratic breed,
And damn an ignorant world
  For differing from the creed.

The Baptists all have hard shells,
  But water is the song,
Little children howl in hell
  Who are not a span long ;
They monopolize the eucharist,
  For them alone given,

Every body's going to hell
  While they go on to heaven;
Rejoice in blissful ignorance,
  Trust to inspiration,
Illiteracy and fanaticism
  Must preach to the nation.

The Methodists, with jovial grace,
  Rejoice in good eatings,
Circuit round from place to place
  And hold protracted meetings,
Take you in on probation,
  Turn you out for pouting,
Start the mission-box around
  When they get 'em shouting;
Sprinkling, pouring, or immersion,
  Just as you take the story—
Only, if you don't fall from grace,
  You'll finally get to glory.

With Campbellites, modern Baptist,
  It's all in the laving,
Unless you are fairly ducked
  To hell you'll go a-staving;
They twist the gospel strangely
  To make their cause out strong,
And by their route to glory
  Ev'ry body is wrong;
As to the gentle spirit,
  They mock its powers given,
Launching their souls in water
  Float calmly on to heaven.

The Universalist's liberal creed
  Makes no long apology,

But sweeps at once a gloomy hell
  From the world's theology;
It makes the best of life and time,
  Profiting by its story,
All the world is saved by grace
  And sweeping on to glory; ·
When through death's dark chilly gloom
  You speed like lightning's flame,
The blood that ope'd heaven's gate
  Closed ev'ry den of shame.

England's church 's a lordly church,
  And sovereign if there 's any,
Sired by uxorious Henry
  In a fit of matrimony;
It has regal patronage,
  Protected by law from strife,
It cut the throat of the good Pope
  To get the king a wife;
Saints of aristocratic caste,
  Its sacerdotal ring,
Have no higher praise for God or man
  Than "Long live the king."

We 'll say naught of Mohammedan
  Nor of Brahminic order,
Though they boast a right divine,
  'T is not upon our border;
Their gods or faiths may serve them,
  But why should we e'er roam,
Who have a God of our own
  And a thousand faiths at home;
Why should we perplex our people
  With foreign innovations,

Whose gods all are strangers
To the genius of our nations?

We'll say naught of Mythology,
In praising or abusing,
Their gods have served out their days,
They are not for modern using;
We admire the poetic skill
That charms each classic page,
But the gods are behind the times,
Our people and our age;
As to the dark Plutonic shore
Where ancient sinners groan,
We'll leave all to antiquity—
We've devil of our own.

The Infidels too have a creed,
The Rationalistic schools,
Where science measures ev'ry thing
By hypothetic rules;
God is squared by a tangent
In arithmetic spasm,
Man's a creature of evolution,
Circumstantial protoplasm;
The baboon's his grandfather,
The jackass is his uncle,
Heaven's made of ginger-bread,
Hell is but a carbuncle.

We'll put all these dogmas in a bag,
Then shake them up and draw,
Risk our chances in the lottery
On the pulling of a straw;
But if perchance we should mistake,
Grim be our melancholy,

The devil will trot us around
  To torture luckless folly,
And deep in hell's sulphurous blaze
  Flaming conscience'll smite one,
As the Terrors hiss and yell,
  " You didn't draw the right one."

YES, I'M A "CORN-CRACKER."

Yes, I'm a " corn-cracker,"
  And I'm proud of my luck,
Bred with the good people
  In the State of old Kentuck;
I boast a loyal pride
  And a reverence profound
For each wild, weird legend
  Of the dark and bloody ground.

I love to recall the story
  Of Boone, the pioneer,
The hardy sons of liberty
  Who followed in his care,
Of brave and dauntless women,
  By tender affections bound,
Who followed their leal lords
  To the dark and bloody ground.

Of many a wild encounter,
  And many a bloody feud
With savage beast and savage men
  In its lonely solitude,
By its wildest rocks and rivers,
  Each valley and each mound,
In the deepest, darkest jungles
  Of the dark and bloody ground.

We Kentuckians are proud
  Of the rough but honest band,
Who through forests tangled and wild
  First pioneered the land;
They were men of nerve and heart,
  The bravest to be found,
Now peacefully rest their bones
  'Neath the dark and bloody ground.

The forests long since cleared away,
  The pioneers gone to rest,
Still the State, broad and ample,
  Peace and plenty blessed,
Has a race of noble men,
  As true as can be found,
Who kindly welcome the stranger
  To the dark and bloody ground.

For the honor of our Nation,
  And its glory for aye,
Many of its bravest sons
  Are wrapped in sacred clay;
And should the Nation call again,
  They will hear its war sound,
For their spirits brood forever
  O'er the dark and bloody ground.

WHY GROW SAD WEARILY THINKING?

Why grow sad wearily thinking, ·
  Dreaming o'er unborn sorrow,
Are there not woes enough present
  To satiate ev'ry horror
Without this fearful foreboding
  Of an evil to-morrow?

True, there are woes in store for all,
  Sad, sad woes of bitter grief!
Who, by anticipating sorrow,
  Can bring the soul relief
Or propitiate evil hours
  That steal on us like a thief?

Some are always repining the past,
  Recounting its bitterest cares,
As if they could erase its woes
  By shedding repentant tears,
Or frighten fate from their doors,
  Parading prophetic fears.

Some in fear are ever dying,
  Living in perpetual dread,
The shroud, the coffin, the dark grave,
  Are always before them spread;
Who has but once in life to die
  Should never die till he's dead.

But who can silence the future,
  Who can e'er forget the past,
Has not man a soul immortal,
  Can he dwarf it like a beast,
Lie down in dumb forgetfulness
  Like the ox after his feast?

Are life's grim ghosts all but phantoms
  To provoke a musing smile?
Is this world only a dreamland
  'Mid shadowy visions wild,
Where all our hopes and all our fears
  Are fictions of fancy's guile?

Oh! lives man not yet again
  In the future, bright or drear,

Has he not a soul immortal,
  *Thrilled by every quick'ning fear,
That struggles for truth within him,
  Teaching his heart to fear?

Still this thought will force upon us:
  Shall we lie down undismayed,
And will the soul like the body
  Crumble back whence it was made,
Is there nothing of man that lives
  When our body has decayed?

Oh! Spirit of the Powers Supreme,
  Inspire our hearts and tell,
Is life but a fleeting dream
  Where vapory shadows dwell,
And are the spectral ghosts of death
  But imagination's hell?

THE SLANDERER.

Arch minion of the Furies,
  Thou fiend of human gore,
The loveliest flower that blooms
  May feel thy blighting power;
Innocence has no protection
  Thy conscience can impart,
Thou 'rt a worm in a rose-bud,
  Feasting on a vital part.

How we shudder when we recall
  All that has e'er been said
Of the tribes of human beings
  Who feed upon their dead;

Darker still the infernal deed,
  Savage and unforgiving,
The bloody fiends in human guise
  Who feed upon the living.

We scorn the miscreant wretches
  Who, in their loathsome toils,
Rob the grave and strip the dead
  To live upon the spoils;
Blacker still and more hellish
  Are the foul fiends of night,
These ghouls who rob innocence
  And strip virtue of its right.

We contemn the vile assassins,
  Mean, mercenary, and bold,
Who steal in the sleeping chamber
  And murder men for gold;
More stealthy the vile serpents
  Who, under virtue's pretence,
Fasten their poisonous fangs
  In the heart of innocence.

THE ABANDONED.

On the river's murky brink
  A wretched woman stood,
Midnight's darkest storm roared
  Above the raging flood;
The same sad tale, faithless love
  And betrayed confidence,
The wiles of human villainy
  And murdered innocence.

She was young and very fair,
  He all her heart desired,
Could his tender, loving eyes
  Be by demons inspired?
Could his soft and gentle smile,
  That fondly thrilled her heart,
Be only a fiendish cloak
  Veiling a hellish part?

But, alas! as sad as true
  Are life's bitter lessons,
Though experience comes late
  To profit by confessions;
Would that some guardian power
  Cleared the darkness round us,
That we might escape the wiles
  Intended to confound us.

Oh! fate, unkind and cruel,
  Where conscience has no rest,
A fiercer storm than roared round
  Was raging in her breast;
Womanhood forc'er blighted,
  Fettered to remorseless shame,
Life's unhappy future dark'ning
  With the world's pitiless blame.

Welcome death, thou sweet solace,
  The shroud and dusky pall,
Woman's hope forc'er blighted,
  Virtue robbed of its all;
Buried in murky waters,
  Where dark and fierce they roll,
Her body to the river sharks,
  To God her wretched soul.

Perhaps, if her heart was known,
　Poor, unfortunate woman,
She yet might find sympathy
　In hearts that are human ;
Wicked man betrays a trust
　In confidence misplaced,
'T is woman's tenderest love
　By which she 's disgraced.

Has poor frail humanity,
　In its deceitful care,
Never for its own weakness
　The semblance of a tear?
Deal gently, my erring brother,
　In every age and clime
Ignorance is the mother
　Of human woe and crime.

IRELAND.

Proud sons of Old Erin, awake
　Your ancient spirit braves !
What rights does England give you?
　Only the rights of slaves;
England, the bloody tyrant,
　Tramples your shamrock low,
Your hands are weak, your hearts are strong,
　You know your crafty foe.

'T is royalty's infernal pride
　And bloody handed might
That, to feast its pompous grandeur,
　Would drape the world in night;

And yet England would talk of slaves
    And curl its lips with scorn,
When every son of Ireland
    Is to its slavery born.

God, curse the pride that would enslave,
    O heaven, protect the free !
What human rights are left to men
    When denied liberty ?
Then 'wake you, sons of Erin, 'wake,
    You know your cunning foe,
If you may not meet it boldly,
    Then strike a stealthy blow.

Old Ireland will yet be free,
    England's power must fail,
Freedom's spirit broods ev'ry land,
    Listening to slavery's wail ;
Despite of kings, despite of lords,
    And rights they call divine,
There are some rights God gives to man
    Which Erin yet will find.

The lords recline on cushioned seats,
    Their conscience light and free,
And when the nation howls for bread
    They call it mutiny ;
The millions toil with flesh-worn hands,
    The lords the fruit consume,
And when they hear gaunt Hunger's wail
    They call it a commune.

The people rise and call on God,
    The king but hears to frown,
And seried ranks of bayonets
    Are sent to hunt them down ;

O, Erin's sons, you have a cause
　　Heaven will surely bless,
'T is well to strike when tyranny
　　Gloats over the oppressed.

We've heard thy cry, O Ireland,
　　Across the surging deep,
And in the freedom of the States
　　We've sat us down to weep;
Our Nation's heart beats wild with hope,
　　Success to Fenian band,
Here Liberty opens wide her arms
　　To every Irishman.

Hither turn, O Erin in exile,
　　Liberty welcomes thee!
Turn from the foul vampire of blood,
　　Come shelter with the free;
The British lion, rampant, in vain
　　Our younger eagle stirred,
But fifty millions of freemen
　　Now guard the full-fledged bird.

THE HOME OF THE POET.

Far from the busy haunts of men,
　　From the world's seething strife,
Alone with Nature in solitude,
　　Breathing the air of life,
Drinking from the sparkling fountains,
　　From Nature's bosom warm,
Resting beneath the forest's shade,
　　Sheltered from sun or storm,

Where Nature spreads her canopy,
  O'er forest, hill, and dale,
Where rippling streams move slowly by,
  Richest perfumes exhale,
Or where the snow-capped mountains stand,
  Giants with hoary locks,
And time 's riven their frozen bows
  With mighty earthquake shocks,

Gentle child of Nature, inspired
  By the wild winds that play,
While ev'ry bird, tree, and flower
  Add melody to thy lay,
Thy home is with the elements,
  The clouds or the sunshine,
The fiercest storms or softest dews,
  Fit companions of thine.

Alone with Nature in her temples,
  A thousand fancies start,
The sweet warblers of the forest
  Pour music in thy heart;
The very wood is filled with song,
  The rustling of the trees
A thousand melodies prolong,
  Rhythmical ev'ry breeze.

Child of Nature, thy proper home
  Is on thy mother's breast,
'T is there thou hast been nourished
  And there must find thy rest;
When thy tuneful lyre is broken
  And the heart-strings are still,
We 'll bury thee in her solitude
  By some soft-murmuring rill.

By the site of thy lonely grave,
　In the shadow of the wood,
The sweetest songsters of the grove
　Will cheer thy solitude;
They will build their nests in the trees
　That stand beside thy grave,
And in the rippling streamlet near
　Their breasts at noontide lave.

DEFEAT.

A cause that's lost in result
　　Must silent be,
　　They're only free
Who are victors to exult.

Success, however won, is sweet
　　To ears of fame,
　　Political shame
The constant factor of defeat.

'T is not always Truth inspiring
　　That leads the strong,
　　Right or wrong,
To shout while the weak are dying!

We're told virtue has a cause
　　God will aright
　　With conscience light
And heaven's smile of sweet applause.

Virtue's cause's a vision flighty,
　　When bristling steel
　　On battle-field
Is the council of the mighty.

Many a barbarous tyrant gory,
    Binding his slaves
    On Freedom's graves,
Tortures them to sing his glory.

Had our cause of Freedom fell,
    Our Washington,
    With trator's doom,
Had languished in a felon's cell.

Had fortune but changed the story,
    Jackson and Lee,
    Traitors they be,
Had filled the world with their glory.

So, in the world's seething strife,
    Fortune's fickle smile
    Wary hearts beguile,
Success weaves the garland crown o' life.

HOW PLEASANT IS THE DREAMING.

How pleasant is the dreaming
    When the summer sun is low,
And the twilight softly streaming
    Thro' the cloud in bright halo!
Where the loveliest flowers bloom
    By the gentle rippling streams
And exhale their rich perfume,
    Very pleasant is the dream.

How we listen to the sounding
    As the bubbling waters move,
Our throbbing hearts still bounding
    To every strain of love;

For we love to dwell where Nature
  Clothes the valley and the hill,
And to drink from ev'ry feature
  Till the soul has drunk its fill.

How our thoughts rise from dreaming
  Up to Nature's God above,
How his bright smiles are beaming
  O'er the world in tender love!
As the glorious sun is sinking
  In the cloudy realm of night,
Our hearts are filled with thinking
  On His grandeur and His might.

Oh! 't is sweet to muse on Nature
  And to dream its visions o'er,
God displayed in ev'ry feature
  In His majesty and power;
In the gentle dew-drops falling
  O'er tender grass and flower,
Or the fierce tornado howling
  In its unbroken power.

SWEET SIXTEEN.

Sweet as the flowers of the orange grove,
Soft as the cooing of the gentle dove,
Fairer than the smiles of beauty's queen,
Is thy maiden dream, O sweet sixteen!

Thy life's as fresh as the budding flower,
Thy heart's as pure as its scented bower,
Ere winter's blast has seared the leaf
Or chilled the tender soul with grief.

My bonny maid, this radiant sheen
Is the canopy of youth's bright dream;
Its hours are winged with pleasure sweet,
Its fairest roses spring 'neath thy feet.

How bright the sky, how sweet the song,
That Nature's harmonies e'er prolong,
Where radiant beauties still unroll
As innocent as thy artless soul!

How soon 't will pass, too soon 't will seem,
For joyous youth with its bright dream,
Then thy fancy can alone restore
These lovely hours that come no more.

THE CONDOR OF THE ANDES.

The condor of the Andes
    Sits high upon the rocks
To prey upon the lambkins
    That stray from out the flocks;
So, even men, like condors,
    With no better pretense,
Prey on the underling herds
    'Gardless of innocence.

And even the proud eagle,
    The king of all the birds,
Sweeps down from his lofty home
    Upon the menial herds;
The eagle, with gory talons,
    Is but a feathered thief,
So human royalty thrives
    Upon the subject's grief. ·

'T is not the eagle alone
　　That essays lofty flights
With the clouds for his home
　　And his nest on the heights,
But the ill-omened vulture,
　　With broadest wings outspread,
Descends from the mountain peaks
　　To feed upon the dead.

Even the loftiest genius,
　　That pinions cloudy fame,
Often stoops like the vulture
　　To lowest depths of shame;
Ever so the arrant pride
　　That boasts a lofty birth.
The vulture, like the eagle,
　　Broods far above the earth.

THERE WAS ONCE A LITTLE FLEDGE-LING.

There was once a little fledgeling,
　　O'er-proud of his knowing,
Who pattern'd from a big shanghai
　　In his strut and crowing.

The shanghai got on a dung-hill
　　To do some tall blowing,
The little chick came creeping out
　　To praise his lord's crowing;

A blue-winged hawk came flying by,
　　Little chick o'erpowered,
Caught him by the tailless parts
　　And quickly him devoured.

Then don't let the bob-tail shanghai,
　Whose praise is all his own,
Entice thee out, my little chick,
　Till thou art older grown;

Wait till you cut your tail-feathers
　Before you try the flight,
And then mount on your own dung-hill
　And crow with all your might;

But while your spurs are very soft
　And shell still to you clings,
Stay snugly in your little nest
　Beneath your mother's wings;

You 'll never know till older grown,
　And retrospective see,
What a damnation little fool
　A small shanghai can be.

LET US BE MERRY WHILE WE LIVE.

Let us be merry while we live,
　And live while yet we may,
This life has little to give,
　And death we can not stay;
　　　Let us be cheery, boys,
　　　Gay and merry, boys,
　　　Never, never weary, boys,
　O'er the uncertainties of the day.

Why need we to go groping,
　Looking for our graves,
Blinded, downcast, and stooping
　Like menial slaves?

Gay hearts beat lightly, boys,
Daily and nightly, boys,
Our sun sets brightly, boys,
Halving life's turbulent waves.

While life is short, the sweeter
Should be its passing hours;
Does sadness make us better
Or wiser in its bowers?
Make the best of life, boys,
Its cares and its strife, boys,
Whatever is rife, boys,
Let it be sunshine and flowers.

And if sorrows need must come,
Can care bring us relief?
Oh! then why disturb our home
With foreshadows of grief!
Let us live or die, boys,
Never, never sigh, boys,
Grief we may not try, boys,
But live while we live—life is brief.

TO THE LOUISVILLE MEDICAL COLLEGE.

O thou, my Alma Mater,
And thou, my Alma Pater!
Equally free;
For my heart knows no other,
Great scientific mother,
Father, sister, or brother,
Only thee.

When as Nature's simple child,
Among her lone rustic wild,
    I have stood
Where shone the gentle sunbeams,
Dancing o'er meadows and streams,
And bright as a fairy's dreams
    All the wood;

Then first in thy massive halls,
In the fair City of the Falls,
    I sought fame;
And when first I thought to roam
From the seclusion of home,
To try alone life's rough storm,
    To thee I came.

Sacred to me are thy halls,
Where medicine rears its walls
    To truth,
Where science with kindling blaze
Spreads round its refulgent rays—
I'll remember thee with the days
    Of my youth.

It is thine ever to impart
Truths to the mind and heart
    Of moral worth;
Like the pilot at his wheel,
Or soldier on battle-field,
To face grim woe, nor e'er yield
    Save to death.

'T is with pride we love to tell
Of those who've faced shot and shell
    On battle-field;
But he is brave who dares stand

Where contagion's unseen hand
Fells its victims o'er the land
　　With flaming steel.

Stays to ease a dying groan—
The next thrust may be his own—
　　Death is rife,
Yet he stays to soothe the smart,
Himself imperil'd, his skill impart,
Humanity with weak'ning heart
　　Pleads for life.

Thy noble art, noble science,
Bids the powers of woe defiance,
　　Superstition flee;
Where in life's flickering shade
Death stands with glass and blade,
Thy votaries, still undismayed,
　　Fight for humanity.

Oh! little knows the world, proud
In its mockery, cruel and loud
　　In its jeers;
Some God only can recompense,
Fighting humanity's defense,
Falling where duty and conscience
　　Alone appears.

They may be kind who have spread
Flowers o'er the harmless dead
　　All undismayed,
Who fled when th' pestilence breath
Filled the land with woe and death,
Every heart, dreading the shaft,
　　Pleading for aid.

When will mankind with discretion
Honor earth's noblest profession,
   ' Faithful from birth?
We praise statesmen and soldier braves,
Each memory with our ensign waves,
But we leave to obscurest graves
   A nobler worth.

The school-boy lisps the bloody fame,
A Napoleon's or Cæsar's name,
   With abated breath,
When 'll Harvey, Jenner, or McDowell
Reap the praise of honest toil?
They 've saved millions from the spoil
   Of grizzly death.

But he who dyes his hands in blood,
And wrecks his country on its flood,
   Is sweet to fame,
Tho' groaning wars like thunders break,
The vanquished wailing at the stake,
Fire and famine follow the wake
   With woe and shame.

O! YE WHO WITH LONG FACES.

O! ye who with long faces
Expect by your sour grimaces
To merit heavenly graces,
   Ye 'ligious breed,
To laugh a burning disgrace is
   By your creed.

Hell was made for the dancer,
The fiddler, and the prancer,

While to heaven ye advance, sirs,
    All profound,
God's greatest glory enchance, sirs,
    When ye frown.

And sure 't is a henious sin
That wicked men should ever grin,
But the devil will take 'em in
    To his nest
Who madly dare to chagrin
    Righteousness.

Is 't 'ligion or disease hepatic
Which, like the fierce vultures emphatic
Tore Prometheus' viscera ecstatic,
    Chained to control,
That makes th' brain a dusty attic
    And sours the soul?

Is it dyspepia with its brood
Of chronic woes, impoverished blood,
Where melancholia in sour mood
    Mounts her thrones
And fills the heart with a flood
    Of weird groans?

Ye've all marked these sour faces
In hypochondriac cases,
Where disease's partner of the graces,
    Life's unpleasant,
Death in shadowy menaces
    Is e'er present.

Pour rich blood into their veins,
Let it course through health, brains,
Rid the nerves of raging pains,
    Clean out the bile;

Nature'll 'wake in mellow strains
With sweetest smile.

'T is not religion, 't is disease,
When man's genial spirits freeze;
Where shifts heaven's softest breeze
　　On velvet cloud,
Joyous Nature, from rocks and trees,
　　Laughs aloud.

BE KIND TO THE LITTLE CHILDREN.

Be kind to the little children,
　　Meet them where or when,
And remember when older grown
　　The boys make the men.

The ragged urchin on the street,
　　Howe'er low his station,
May preside o'er the republic,
　　The pride of our Nation ;

The white-haired boy behind the plow
　　Is in the hands of fate,
His voice may wake the nations round
　　From out the halls of State ;

The dirty newsboy on the street,
　　The bootblack in the alley,
May lead the armies of the brave
　　When Freedom bids 'em rally.

Teach the boys pure lessons,
　　May they be true and brave,
Love the memories of their fathers,
　　The rights they died to save.

17

Teach them that truth and virtue
Befits for every station,
That they 're the hopes of Liberty,
Bulwarks of the Nation.

TO THE COMMITTEE

Who came to inquire why I should not be dismissed from the Baptist Church for certain heterodox opinions. It is needless to say that I went out by a large majority.

Gentlemen of the committee,
It is a great pity
   That we should disagree
In this land of churches,
Where truth in its searches
   Finds ev'ry conscience free.

As to Abraham or Moses,
The contour of their noses
   Is of little worth to me;
All your doctrinal cavil
But opens for the devil
   A big hole in theology.

Thank God, this age of reason
Makes it no longer treason
   If we should disagree;
The bloody Inquisition
Has no more a mission
   For the sons of Liberty.

A brighter day is dawning,
All hail! the glorious morning,
   Farewell your priestly knaves;
Hearts of virtuous bravery

Scorn the menial slavery
That binds them in its caves.

'T is a shabby faith, indeed,
That prescribes a certain creed
  To fetter Almighty God,
Where mortal men 're sinking
For the very thinking
  Their hearts fail to accord.

Yet you talk so sprightly,
Really, you delight me
  Beyond poetic measure;
The great God is chartered,
Salvation has been bartered,
  To suit schismatic pleasure.

Oh! who would narrow his soul
To the bigoted control
  Proscribing dogmas have given;
Rather let him converse
With God, his universe
  Limitless love and heaven.

No, God is fettered by rules,
Man must be taught in schools,
  How to approach his throne,
Nor is the untutored thought
Simple prayer of the heart,
  Only a wasted groan.

Is God the God of isms,
Does he delight in schisms,
  Rich churches in haughty pride,
Or yet has he no haunt,
Save where ignorance and want
  Boast what thriftless hands denied?

Has the great God partial friends
To whom a special light descends,
   Revealing all eternity,
While other hearts are clouded
And other hopes are shrouded
   In mystic uncertainty?

But when we make our searches,
In which of all the churches
   Is the shekinah burning?
Oh! where is the solid rock
The gates of hell will ne'er shock
   Until our Lord's returning?

Good-bye, messieurs committee,
Neither your grace or pity
   Need ye reserve for me,
I would not give my old socks
For all your creeds orthodox;
   Thank God, I'm mentally free.

Free from priest, creeds, and schisms blind,
Free in heart and free in mind,
   I grasp Mercy by the hand;
The world's too large to be proscribed,
God's love too rich to e'er be bribed
   By any priestly clan.

If naught but Baptists get to heaven,
How small will be the earthly leaven
   In that great country blessed!
I'll sit me down on a dung-hill,
And tune my harp to discord shrill,
   Till every soul finds rest.

If only the few are to be blessed,
Send me to hell with all the rest

When I quit this mortal site;
'Mid flowers or flames, where'er God sends,
Only let me be with my friends,
    And my soul will delight.

But grander hopes I have for man,
A grander God to rule the land
    And soothe the soul oppressed;
Wherever throbs the human heart,
Its swelling anthems upward start
    And find in Him a rest.

GAZE ON THE DUSKY FACE OF DEATH.

Gaze on the dusky face of Death,
    Mark the glazed and shrunken eye,
The soul slumbers no more beneath,
    All the streams of life are dry;
Cold and expressionless the face,
    Dark and swollen lips betide
No more of glory or disgrace,
    Sleep senseless of human pride.

Where is the flick'ring flame of life
    That set these dull eyes aglow,
Kindled dark passions into strife,
    Filled the soul with bitter woe,
Woke the mind to immortal reason,
    Thrilled the heart with hope and love,
Banished evil thoughts like treason,
    Centering all on God above?

Where's the soul-principle immortal,
    Who saw it take its wing'd flight

Upward to celestial portal—
　Downward in the gloomy night?
It has gone; life and soul 've fled,
　Fierce passions no longer rife,
We 're gazing on the solemn dead,
　Gazing on the debris of life.

Little profits now the learning
　Spread o'er wisdom's ample page,
Stilled the powers of discerning,
　Silent is ambition's rage;
All of earthly fame and glory
　Fading in this moldering heap,
Few shall ever hear his story
　Or care to disturb his sleep.

But what if earth's sovereigns bow
　Suppliants before his shrine,
Can Death be flattered by mere show
　Or enthused by praise divine?
Will the grave repeat his fame
　Or soothe its long, dreary hours,
If millions should exalt his name
　And wreathe his memory with flowers?

No lingering line e'er leaves its trace
　Upon the visage of Death,
Deeds of honor or disgrace
　Vanish with the fleeting breath;
Prophetic of another world,
　We stand by life's dusky river,
The dark waves lash in madd'ning whirl,
　Man sinks and 's lost forever.

THE LAWYERS.

Reaped by the ruthless scythe of time,
  The old farmer's no more;
But by thrift and economy
  He left some means in store
To save the family from charity
  And the wolf at the door.

Worse by far than the hungry wolf
  Is that ungenerous fate,
Where avaricious lawyers feed
  Upon the dead man's estate,
Drinking the widow's groans and tears
  To quench a thirst insatiate.

The widow's cries are piteous   ·
  And the famished wolf mourns,
He's watching the legal ghouls
  Torturing bereaved groans,
Waiting till the vampires leave,
  Then he will pick the bones.

In little costs and little fees
  The foul crime is begun,
The estate melts like winter's snow
  Before a summer's sun;
Soon not a trace will be left,
  When the lawyers are done.

Is there no power yet supreme,
  Will Mercy never speak?
Is there no protecting arm
  To guard the innocent weak
And save the widow and orphans
  From the law's cruel beak?

Abominable harpies! foul birds,
  Ye feed upon the dead,
The quivering hearts of the living
  Are round your tables spread,
Ye are fat from human gore
  For your luxury shed.

AS TO THE SPECIAL CREED.

As to the special creed,
With apostles agreed
  And John Baptist firm on,
We'll leave to the fighters,
The schismatic biters,
Theological writers,
  And let them determine.

As to the orthodox,
They are like chicken cocks
  Contending for the barn-yard,
Who shall boss the hens,
Who shall scratch the pens,
The how's to crow and when's
  To exactly please the Lord.

The fools fight for creeds,
Wise men are for deeds
  Ever firmest debaters;
The priests are all a sham,
They do not care a d—n
Save for the eggs and ham,
  Chicken and potatoes.

The churches are but schools
Wherein they train fools
   To pay tribute to preachers;
The priests do the scouting,
The women do the shouting,
And the rich shell out then;
   Oh! they are merry creatures.

The priests tell the story,
Giving God all glory,
   But selfish ends discerning;
The priests eat the honey,
The priests get the money,
And fools think it's funny
   Thus to spend their earning.

With angelic complexion
They take up a collection
   When the Lord is short of change,
Then, to make you even,
Give you a check on heaven,
Securing what you've given
   In celestial exchange.

If you'd test the preacher
As any other creature,
 · Thus try the sacred scholar,
Test him by this fashion:
Strike him on his ration,
You'll find his holy passion
   Is measured by the dollar.

THE GODS.

High on his great Olympic throne
  Jove majestically reclined,
Ancient Rome and classic Greece
  Bowed suppliants at his shrine;
From his dark brow the black'ning storms
  Maddened before his breath,
And lightnings flashed and thunders roar'd,
  The earth trembled beneath.
But the Thunderer loved his people,
  And, with his ensign unfurled,
Ancient Rome and classic Greece
  Ruled all the then-known world
Till Frank and Goth with fiery gods,
  War-like and infernal,
O'erthrew Olympus and its powers
  With all its gods eternal;
So Rome and Greece are now no more,
  Save in classic diction,
The prowess of their mighty gods
  Survives only in fiction.

In ancient Israel, we are told,
  Jehovah was respected,
And from Sinai's flaming heights
  Her martial hosts directed;
Forth from the flames he flashed his laws,
  Swelling in thunder tones,
The trembling mountain shook with fear,
  Nature convulsed in groans;
Enthroned upon a blazing cloud,
  With vapory spear all gory,
He swept before them like a storm
  And led them on to glory;

But His people fore'er scattered,
   His grandeur long since flown,
IIis temple has been pillaged
   And prestige overthrown ;
All his ancient powers humbled,
   E'en as the gods of Rome,
He lives only on a pension
   Bequeathed him by his son.

So gods, like empires, crumble
   Before the breath of time,
A nation rises but to pass away
   With all its gods sublime.
Where now is Egypt or Chaldea,
   Lineages of learned priest,
Gods that gave them wealth and power,
   Promising never to cease ?
Through thousands of circling years
   Men bowed before Osiris,
With faith bright they sought his aid,
   Dying, entered his paradise ;
Many whisperings from spirit-land,
   Breathed by prophet, priest, or sage,
Told how the powers behind the clouds
   Would rule in every age ;
Still the searing blast of time
   Humbled these ancient powers,
Shook their fierce gods from out the clouds
   And 's given place to ours.

To-day, where living empires move,
   Mighty arms shake sea and land,
Other gods have been enthroned
   Suited to present demand ;

Buddha, Brahma, Mahomet, Christ,
  Great gods of mighty nations,
While the present empires last
  Will ne'er lose their occupations.
But as the ruthless course of time
  Rolls on in centuries' flight,
'T will leave the nations in decay,
  Histories in forgotten night,
Other nations and other gods
  Will survive our long decay,
And wonder on the strange people
  Who lived in our day;
As they worship their living gods
  They will fable out our own,
Marking each sad infatuation
  Binding us to gods unknown.

TRUTH AND RIGHT.

Oh! may we learn truth
  From nature's ample page,
The tinted bloom of youth,
  The seared leaf of age,
For ev'ry hour imparts
  This saddest confession,
The errors of our hearts
  Form life's bitter lesson.

Eternal truth and right
  Will survive the powers
Of iron-handed might
  Tho' crushed like frail flowers,
They will bloom in the heart
  Of virtuous and brave,

Waiting life's spring to start
From winter's frosty grave.

They may be crushed by hate
Where hypocrisy's smiles,
As by an unseen fate,
Lend aid to wicked guiles;
But like lovely flowers
Our genial thoughts impart
Love's mellowing showers
To the growth of the heart.

A host of wicked schemes
May thrive on innocence,
Until all virtue seems
Without human defense;
Retribution will come,
However long delayed,
When like the maddening storm
Its wrath can not be stayed.

Innocence will find rest
Hope and faith have given,
Above life's raging blast,
'Neath the smiles of heaven;
Fond hope, 't is ample pay
To bosoms leal and true,
Nearing eternity
We bid this world adieu.

While we live, still recall,
With each vapory breath,
Time has mortgaged its all
To the powers of death;
Life's but a meteor's blaze,
Only a flash of light,
Black clouds engulf its rays
And darker grows the night.

OUR COUNTRY, AND OUR COUNTRY'S FLAG.

Our country, and our country's flag,
　　Unfurl the stars and stripes beside
Where freemen shout in triumph loud,
　　Rejoicing in a Nation's pride;
Home of the great, land of the free,
　　Washed in the blood of patriot braves,
Long may thou stand a beacon light
　　To warn the tyrant and his slaves!

The shrill voice of Patrick Henry
　　Thrills us from the land of dream,
The blood of Lexington and Concord
　　Pours fore'er a crimson stream;
Immortal sons of Liberty,
　　Who scorned to be England's slaves,
Can we e'er dishonor the flag
　　That yet floats above their graves?

Look toward Bunker's blood-stain'd hill,
　　Where towers 'loft our marble pride,
There Warren fell, and there his blood
　　Still swells Freedom's glorious tide;
See Valley Forge's dismal camp,
　　And live its bitter winters o'er,
There mark the foot-prints of Freedom
　　In bloody tracks thro' ice and snow.

We honor our illustrious dead,
　　We hallow their sacred graves;
Shall we not love our country
　　As we love its patriot braves?

May we not cherish the fond hope
   The Union will forever stand,
And Liberty ope wide her arms
   To the slaves of ev'ry land?

Cursed be the treachery of Arnold!
   Black be his living disgrace,
Who can be tempt'd by British gold
   To sell his country's hope and peace!
A stench in the nostrils of Freedom,
   A foul putrescent odor,
That leaves him to enjoy alone
   The base title of traitor.

How glorious our Washington,
   Whose memory none can e'er deride,
At whose shrine a Nation bows,
   Whose life is his country's praise;
Fifty millions of true freemen,
   Who never bowed the servile knee,
Are ready with their arms and wealth
   To defend his memory.

High unfurl our streaming banner,
   Freemen, rally to its side,
Tho' baptized in blood and fire
   Still it is the Nation's pride;
May ne'er the land of Washington,
   That Arnold could not betray,
Be less the land of hope and pride,
   God's chosen land of Liberty.

Proud kings, with self-imposed glory
   Man's natural rights you have spurned,
Look to the land where all are free,
   Where every wandering eye is turned,

Hear Freedom's loud exultant shout
  Swelling in mighty thunder tones,
Shaking the empires of the earth
  And tottering imperial thrones!

WILD OATS.

He sowed wild oats with liberal hand,
Regardless of the soil or sand,
Sowed in vice and reaped in grief;
The harvest passed without relief,
The winter came in raging blast,
Howling over profligate waste;
So age creeps on with pitiless ruth'
To mock the days of wasted youth.

Joyous youth in its rosy prime
Promised perpetual spring time,
It seemed as if its sun-lit hours
Would glide fore'er 'mid lovely flowers,
Where balmy clouds and gentle dews
O'er nature wide their charms diffuse,
Until the world all seemed, forsooth,
But life's perennial spring of youth.

But Eldorado's famous fountain
Gushes no more from ancient mountain,
No more its streams of youth are spread,
Its plains are dry, its flowers dead.
Ye withered crones, now read the truth,
Youth is its own fountain of youth,
A few short years its beauty streams,
Then fades away like fancy's dreams.

Youth oft' drinks of folly's draught,
Though poisonous ev'ry drink quaffed,
Pleasure's environed with sorrows
Where death tips a thousand arrows;
Fools, attrac'd by show and glitter,
Reap life's experience bitter,
But wisdom, crowned by common sense,
Profits by fool's experience.

THE PILGRIM FATHERS.

On Plymouth's dreary rock
    The Pilgrim Fathers landed,
Who in a common cause
    A common fate had banded;
For freedom of conscience
    They plowed the stormy sea,
To plant on a frozen shore
    The germ of Liberty.

Upon a rugged rock,
    'Mid winter's howling groan,
Roughly hewn honest hearts
    Erected Freedom's throne,
Through years of sorest trials
    Tyranny's shocks withstood,
Consecrating the soil
    With their own sacred blood.

Little dreamed the toil-worn few,
    Struggling 'gainst the Fates,
They were in Freedom's halls,
    In the proud realm of States,

That God would build a home
  To shelter the oppressed,
Where Freedom fore'er would smile
  On ev'ry human breast.

O God, bless the May Flower!
  Long may its name survive,
And glorious States yet unborn
  Keep its memory alive;
For when Freedom's voice called
  Her sons to rise and arm,
The Pilgrims responded
  Nobly to the alarm.

WE HAVE MET AND WE HAVE PARTED.

We have met and we have parted,
  The last farewell has been spoken,
The vows of love that bound us
  Are now forever broken;
My bosom's filled with anguish,
  My soul with passion is bound,
My heart is bleeding strangely,
  Bleeding from its secret wound.

We had quarreled, as lovers will,
  Mindless of contention's shroud,
For I was frigid and formal
  And she was haughty and proud;
Well, I thought that she loved me,
  That her heart was leal and true;
Once she smiled as if relenting,
  Then coolly bid me adieu.

She was the idol of my heart
  And was to have been my bride,

Only a foolish little jest
  Poisoned our souls with its pride;
But one word, one smile, or one look
  Had spared the broken-hearted,
And all would have been forgiven
  And we had never parted.

I'll send her back her letters,
  Their presence strangely grieves me,
I'll tell her I've forgotten all,
  Perhaps she will believe me;
But I'll keep this lock of hair
  To remember its pleasures,
She's forgotten it, no doubt,
  Tho' greatest of my treasures;

I'll keep this little rose-bud too,
  Its memories are so bright,
She pinned it on my coat one eve
  When kissing me a good-night;
And this little bunch of cedar,
  It fills my heart with pain,
She told me that she'd love me
  Till I returned it again;

This bouquet of forget-me-nots
  I guard with tenderest care,
I have kept as a souvenir
  Since I clipped it from her hair;
She told me passions were fatal,
  If ever I felt their grief
To send it back to her again,
  She'd come to my relief.

But when by its haughty pride
  The frail human soul is bound,

Even though the heart's bleeding
  It tries to conceal its wound;
So I will nurse my sorrow,
  None shall ever hear my groan,
The fierce pains that tear my heart
  Will be forever unknown.

I have met her on the street,
  She passes silently by,
No gentle smile upon her face
  Nor glistening tear in her eye;
As cold as the marble slab
  Indexing a quiet grave,
I pass her as I would the dead,
  And yet I am her slave.

But sometimes I meet her now
  In the fancy of my dreams,
Where passions are not deceptive
  And love is all that it seems,
In my fancy catch her smile
  With its thousand sunny rays,
Where soft eyes are beaming love
  As they used in other days.

ON RECEIVING NOTICE THE CHURCH HAD EXCOMMUNICATED ME FOR HET-ERODOXY.

Old Zion's ship is coursing on,
  'Mid the stormy waves and gales,
They've flung the poet overboard
  Like Jonah among the whales;

But his soul is still undaunted,
   'Mid life's ocean, surging dark,
He rides the monsters of the deep
   And chases the raging shark;

When the tempest clouds all vanish
   And truth's golden light breaks through,
You'll find him still upon the wave,
   Still "paddling his own canoe."

All the nations will join the song,
   Nor Inquisitions gory
Drive mankind to a fiery hell
   And shut the gates of glory;

Election must go to the bad,
   Hell yet will bloom with roses,
When kings and priests take to the plow
   And prejudice reposes.

OH! OUR BOYS DREAM OF JOYS.

Oh! our boys dream of joys
   When they flirt the girls,
      But believe me,
      They'll deceive thee,
      They'll grieve thee,
   If thou pull their curls.

It's charming, not alarming,
   To kiss their pretty beaks;
      Can't refute it,
      Don't dispute it,
      Just impute it
   To their blushing cheeks.

Be careful, e'en prayerful,
  Love 's a two-edged dart;
    Though it 's fun, sir,
    When begun, sir,
    Ere thou 'rt done, sir,
  Thou 'lt have lost thy heart.

It is pleasing, cooing, teasing,
  Flirting the charming girls;
    Sweet and fair, sir,
    Then take care, sir,
    And beware, sir,
  There 's danger in the curls.

A TOAST—THE WINE.

Here, by our friendship eternal,
  Is to the blood of the grape,
Here we scorn powers infernal
  And destiny's evil shape;
Oh! would to God no greater woe
  Human conscience e'er belied;
Oh! would that crime, all crimson'd o'er,
  By deeper stain was ne'er dyed.
Beside, I 've a secret to disclose,
  To you I 'll freely make it:
They all take it under the rose,
  Blessed or cursed—they all take it.

A TOAST—WOMAN AND WINE.

Here's food for heart and food for brain,
　A surcease from human strife,
An antidote for ev'ry bane
　That poisons the stream of life;
A surfeit of love leads to loathe,
　A surfeit of wine to decay,
We'll mix life's cup gently with both
　And we'll be happy alway.

TO ROBERT INGERSOLL.

Ah! Bob, dear Bob, thou'st done a deal
　With strange talk and visions flighty,
As if the world was one small field
　And thou thyself God Almighty;
Thou hast told us, Bob, there's no hell
　To open wide its grim portals,
No devil in his dusky cell
　Torturing souls of immortals;

Thou'st prated 'bout father Adam
　And great-grandmother Eve " to boot,"
Thou'st told that 't is all a sham,
　This talking snake and mortal fruit;
Then there was one pious Moses
　At whom thy wicked puns thou poke,
And so old Sinai reposes
　All in the shadow of thy joke.

Through ev'ry sacred field of glory
　Thou'st plow'd with dirty satire,
Waded through life's eternal story
　As if 't was only filthy mire;

Thou 'st torn wide the nation's heart,
  Disturbed society's repose,
As if thou 'd other gods to impart,
  Other religions to disclose;

Thou 'st ridiculed old Balaam's ass,
  Thou 'st said 't was all a joke,
These legends of the fabled past,
  When the snakes and asses spoke;
Thou 'st derided the patriarchs hoary,
  From old Noah's big floating tub
To Joshua's great sun-story,
  And chariots with flaming hub;

Thou hast laughed at faithful Daniel,
  Mocked his holy prayer toward Zion,
As if his den held a spaniel,
  Not a carniverous lion;
Even old Jonah and his gourd
  Have felt thy vengeance gory,
As if credence could not afford
  To swallow just one fish-story.

The prophets, seers, and the preachers,
  All have felt thy subtle shaft,
Painted up as cunning creatures
  Or fossils at whom to laugh.
Thou 'st made the church and its steeple
  Only emissaries of the graves,
Wherein the priests herd the people
  And frighten tribute out of slaves;

Thou 'st told us, Bob, that priestly craft
  Arrayed earth in its present plight—
In our sleep sometimes we 've laughed
  And half dreamed thou art right;

But then, dear Bob, heaven, you know,
 Is to th' elect a thing o' beauty,
And hell, if but an old scare-crow,
 Drives the recreant to duty.

Now, Bob, e'en grant that thou art right,
 And for once we 'll not dispute it,
Would not society be a fright
 If all believed as thou impute it?
Shall we throw around society
 No restraint to guard its border?
If virtue needs no spur to piety,
 Vice must be driven to order.

But then, dear Bob, there 's many a wrong
 That well might be arighted,
The weak 's oppressed, and e'en the strong
 By cunning knaves affrighted;
In ev'ry land, in ev'ry clime,
 The vast millions are distressed,
Exempt from tax but not from crime,
 A few enslave all the rest.

FOR HEARTS THAT ARE LEAL AND TRUE.

The clouds are lifting from out the morning,
 The light is streaming through,
A brighter and better day is dawning
 For hearts that are leal and true.

Steady, my friends, nor e'er swerve from the line,
 Conscience is a plummet sure,
The right will survive all the wrongs of time
 For hearts that are leal and true.

When with death are numbered all now alive,
    And their graves are wet with dew,
The memory of noble deeds will survive
    For hearts that are leal and true.

The future will judge though flatterers applaud,
    The lives of all 't will review,
When the slanderer sleeps in his silent shroud
    Nor maligns the leal and true.

Then strive for the right, but not like a slave
    Who is bribed or driven through,
The hypocrite has an inglorious grave,
    Never hearts that 're leal and true.

HYPOCRISY.

How oft' religion's fair masks
    Disguise the Devil's face
Until he performs his tasks,
    Thus sheltered from disgrace.
Oh! wretched dissembling guile,
    Even virtue's cause bleeds,
Devils with angelic smiles
    Clothe their infernal deeds.
Religion's oft but a cloak
    To hide some monster sin,
Black vice with wrinkled visage,
    Crouching with fiendish grin,
A mean, subtle, lurking foe,
    On foulest crimes intent,
A snare to the unsuspecting,
    Unwary, and innocent.

THE MURKY CLOUDS WERE LOWERING.

The murky clouds were lowering
    O'er forest, field, and glen,
When in fancy I wandered forth
    To view the cares of men ;
The winter, black and menacing,
    Gathered in all its wrath,
From clouds of snow and streams of ice
    Frowned darkly on my path.

The world seemed like a busy hive
    Filled with honeyed treasures,
And men, like bees, were buzzing round
    Searching for its pleasures ;
Some had merry faces and hearts,
    Despising woes and cares,
While others, weighed down with sorrows,
    Trembled always with fears.

Some, with faces as fair as the morn,
    Lived for gayest digressions,
And some, all sore and forlorn,
    Like sad funeral processions ;
Some dwelled alone with the living,
    Where fairest hours are spread,
Others lived among old graveyards,
    Fit companions of the dead ;

Some moved through life in easy paths,
    Treasures strewn where'er they stray,
While others, straining ev'ry nerve,
    Scarce could drive the wolf away ;
Ev'ry thing some touched was gold,
    The philosopher's stone theirs,

Yet others, equally alert,
　　Were fed on beggars' prayers;

Some dwelled in stately mansions grand,
　　All with human pride inspired,
Where Plenty with her lavish hand
　　Heaped what the heart desired;
Some hard by, in wretched huts
　　'Neath shadows of lordly waste,
Gaunt with hunger and poorly clad,
　　Shivered in the wintry blast;

Some too seemed favorites of health,
　　Disease relenting its ruth,
The ruddy glow upon the cheeks
　　Marked its perpetual youth,
Others, infected from their birth,
　　From maternal bosoms warm,
Disease through life with vicious breath
　　Haunted to pain and deform;

Some, formed symmetrical and erect,
　　Easy in manners and grace,
Were perfect pictures of manhood
　　Typed in mind and in the face,
Others only freaks of nature;
　　Some were deaf, some dumb, some blind,
Or hideous in ev'ry aspect
　　Elevating to human kind;

Some Nature with intellects endowed,
　　Generous favor, the cultured mind,
Standing forth lords of creation
　　Where reason rules, all sublime;
Some decreed idiots and imbeciles,
　　Born to the lowest repute,

Without e'en the semblance of minds,
　　Lower than the dullest brute.

Even in the vacillant taste,
　　Capacity to enjoy life,
Nature still had its favorite pets
　　Protected in ev'ry strife;
There's not a sphere in which men move,
　　Nor boon to mortals given,
Save where Nature with partial grace
　　Meted out its hell or heav'n.

No wonder that the human mind
　　Is shocked with grief and fears,
When we look round the world its smiles
　　Are mingled all with tears;
The few are born to golden luck,
　　The millions are distressed,
And ev'ry path of pleasure leads
　　O'er prostrate and oppressed.

WE'VE LAID HIM AWAY IN A COLD, COLD GRAVE.

We've laid him away in a cold, cold grave,
　　A rough slab at his head,
His soul is gone, God only knows where—
　　We only know he's dead.

The face that met us always with smiles,
　　Smiles in death, and it seems,
So natural his look, he only slept
　　Wrapped in pleasant dreams.

As time courses on and the years roll by
  Till his memory's faded,
Who will distinguish his scattered dust
  From dust where we've laid it?

Let seers and prophets and priests now tell
  What ancient legends said
Of the veil rent in the mystic realm—
  We only know he's dead.

BEAUTY AND GRACE MEN SELDOM DERIDE.

Beauty and grace men seldom deride,
Excepting those to whom denied;
Ill-favored genius scorns their power,
But, like the fox, the grapes are sour,
And oft poor and humble worth
Contemns titled grandeurs of earth.
'T is well that each heart can impeach
The pleasures far beyond its reach,
And press home the consolation,
Itself a favorite of creation;
'T is well that the plebeian can sing,
"God digged a hell to damn the king."
Ignorance moral exemption claim,
What man never knew who can blame?
Fools hold the wise in resentment,
That all may live blessed with contentment.

THE BACKWARD SPRING OF 1881.

Oh! gentle, mellow, balmy spring,
　Many hearts it has cheered,
Still in winter's arms it clings,
Flopping 'bout with snowy wings
　And frost upon its beard.

The frogs croak by the ice-pond,
　The ground-hog's hibernating,
With frozen hearts we look on,
Listening to its plantive song,
　Sadly prognosticating.

The swallow and the robin
　Have come without the flowers,
No cheering bosoms throbbing,
Bleak winter still absorbing
　Nature's verdant powers.

The snakes and beetles dormant,
　The crickets refuse to sing,
No other beast or varmint,
Save man alone in torment,
　Is waiting for the spring.

Carry us to the apothecary,
　We'll all get drunk together;
In this world bleak and dreary
Man can find enough to weary
　Without troubling the weather.

Here's health to the poets of spring,
　To all who love a rhyme;
As our voices gladly ring,
Fill the cups with cheer we bring,
　And drink health to the spring time.

A CRUEL TAUNT, A SIMPLE JEST.

A cruel taunt, a simple jest,
May rancor in the human breast,
Thoughtless words, unguarded spoken,
Friendship's strongest ties have broken;
For little words, like little weeds,
Smother the growth of better deeds.

Gentle smiles confidence impart,
Kind feelings warm the chilly heart,
Simple words but softly spoken
Heal the heart by sorrow broken;
So little flowers do exhume
When fully grown richest perfume.

Then from these truths a lessons learn,
·All silly words and actions spurn,
For little words are mighty things
When joy or grief each passion brings,
Roughly wounding or gently healing
When applied to human feeling.

TO THE EXILED EMPRESS EUGENIE, OF FRANCE.

Wretched woman, by cruel fate
Torn from the throne of regal state,
Must France bow a menial slave
To save thee from a plebeian grave?

Shall claims of blood and titled birth
Exalt thee to unmerited worth,
To pomp and show and vain delights
Bought at the price of human rights?

The world marks with curious smile
The tears of monarchs in exile
Pleading for sovereignty of nations,
Power once held by usurpations.

Well may Liberty's sons deride,
And jeering mock thy Bourbon pride,
Condemning millions to distress
That thou might be an empress.

Is human pride so far debased,
Liberty's butchered for mere caste,
And Freedom condescends to sing
In servile lays, "Long live the king?"

Thinkest thou not that slaves have groans
As well as monarchs without thrones?
Must human tears flow in deep tide
To fill the hearts of lordly pride?

Oh! curse the fate that has given
Mankind no rights 'neath the heaven
But to be born in menial brood,
Slaves to aristocratic blood.

Is it better France, like a slave,
Be bound in chains on Freedom's grave,
Or that her exiled monarch sleep
And queen for regal splendors weep?

Oh! Liberty, extend thy light
To ev'ry land in slavery's night,
Till ev'ry throne's a fun'ral pile
And every monarch an exile;

Unfurl thy flag above each dome,
Protect the rights of ev'ry home,
Teach mankind that truest bravery
Prefers death rather than slav'ry.

OLD MARGARET DUNN, THE WITCH,
AND PARSON JONES.

Old Margaret Dunn, of Stoner's creek,
Of whom our county legends speak,
No mongrel blood flowed thro' her veins,
Nor sympathy for human banes;
She was a witch, a witch indeed,
A stalwart of the noblest breed,
Hers the papers, as all could tell,
Signed by the sovereign prince of hell,
Commissioned by infernal right
To work her charms day and night.
　　Old Marg. lived in a hovel poor,
All thatched with straw, of earth the floor,
Which hung upon a cliff above,
Like a rude box or cote for dove;
But Margaret was a fright to see,
Old and stooped and wrinkled was she,
Bald as an owl, and toothless yet
Till her nose and chin almost met,
Blear-eyed and mean for meanness sake,
A witch she was without mistake.
　　Now, Parson Jones lived in the glen:
The parson was the best of men,
A Methodist of the old school,
Who'd pray and shout by love-feast rule;
It was the good parson's delight
To say his prayers both day and night,
" Since Hardin Stallers, strong and stout,
Left Black Lick and Stoner out."
Now twice each month, when Sunday reached,
He at Black Lick and Stoner preached;

From ev'ry hill and ev'ry ranch,
Robinson's creek and Dutton's branch,
Came rustic lads and blooming lasses,
Both old and young in seried masses,
To hear the parson's well-tuned sound
Wake all the hills with echoes round.

But Parson Jones was sore distressed,
One thought forever broke his rest,
Where'er he went, whate'er his mission,
He saw old Marg.'s apparition;
Her spectral self hung round his way,
Haunting his dreams both night and day,
Nor had he power of mind or arms
To stay her cunning or her charms.

Some said the parson's mind was weak,
Some said that he was only sick,
But nostrums much nor prayer profuse
His wretched soul could disabuse;
Not indigestion's wicked banes
That racked his bones at morn with pains,
It was old Marg., who, by her spell,
Had ridden him o'er hill and dell.

When first old Marg. the parson met,
They both were free and sinless yet;
'T is true she had her black commission,
But he was not in its mission.

Now, old Marg. on a forage went,
On bird or fowl or pig intent,
But, luckless for the parson's peace,
Fell into a flock of his geese;
Now, Parson Jones, in Scripture way,
Was on the " watch as well as pray,"
He bounced old Marg. with courage true
And beat the wench till black and blue;

When this she said, hobbling away :
" Ah, Parson Jones, thou 'lt rue this day ;
I 'll send disease and hawk and owl,
Thou 'lt never raise a goose or fowl,
Thou 'lt curse the day and hour, son,
Thou laidst thy hand on Margaret Dunn."
True to her threat, that very day
The hawks and owls commenced their prey,
And all they left from perch or shed
Dropped one by one and fell down dead ;
When all were dead save one old goose,
The parson sat with thoughts morose,
The old goose flopped close to his side,
Uttered a groan, fell down and died.

At home sat Marg. with bitter heart,
Brewing her charms in hellish art,
Weaving in grief with dire groans
And vengeance for old Parson Jones ;
Not yet enough, what witch 's content
Or to mercy can e'er relent,
If for lost fowls only he groans,
He yet shall wail for his own bones.

Now, Parson Jones had heard it said,
If one would burn the witched when dead,
Despite of all her cunning care
The guilty witch would straight appear ;
Scarce sunk the last goose to repose
When in the fire her carcass goes,
And scarce the flames the fowl spread o'er,
Old Margaret stepped within the door.

Parson, she said, with right good will,
Loan me your horse to ride to mill ;
Begone, he said, thou demon base,
Out of my house, off of my place,

Nor grace my sight, nor ever more
Bring thy mean form within my door;
What needs devil or witch for nag,
Go ride thy broom, thou wretched hag!
Parson, she said, I'll bend thy pride,
I'll go this night, and I will ride
As noble steed as ever queen
Rode on the mission of a fiend.
Casting on him a wicked glare,
She left him with a queenly air.
   The Parson barred his doors that night,
Unchained his dogs, his guns rubbed bright,
Picked the flint and powdered the pan,
Placed his best ax ready for hand;
On the Bible a tallow light
Burned dimly the dreary night,
He read and prayed and, singing, roared
Till heavy sleep his limbs o'erpowered.
True to her threat, old Margaret came,
The dogs all cowed before her tame,
She greased a straw with magic grease,
And slipped thro' the key-hole with ease,
Bridled the parson with silk thread
And gently drove him out of bed.
As to the parson, he but dreamed,
For through his sleep her magic streamed;
He dreamed himself on a tour,
Black Lick would get a sermon sure.
As to old Marg., with magic cold
She drove her steed through the key-hole,
And mounting, like an airy sprite,
She spurred the courser on his flight;
Over hills and hollows far and wide,
O'er miry bogs and raging tide,

Through briars, bushes, and rough places
She drove him on in weary paces;
And thus she rode the live-long night,
Urging her steed to better flight,
But brought him home ere it was light
And placed him on his couch aright;
But ere she left, she whispering spoke,
" Old Marg.'s been here!"   Straight he awoke—
But never a trace of the old crone,
Save matted hair and aching bone.
Thus ev'ry night the old witch came,
And ev'ry night rode him the same,
And each time whispered in his ear:
" Parson Jones, old Marg.'s been here."
Thus, till all strength and courage fled,
Nor could he rise next day from bed;
Slow pining 'way with quick'ning breath,
Old Marg. had rode him to his death.

OH! FILL UP THE BOWL AND PASS IT AROUND.

Oh! fill up the bowl and pass it around,
  We'll drink to the health o' the living;
Quietly our fathers sleep in the ground,
  Unconscious of life's misgiving.
    Why dream ye of fear?
    Why mourn over care?
    In the wine or beer
The sorrows of life ye may drown.

Let teetot'lers sing of the sparkling wave
  Filled with beauty and happiness bright,

Have we in our midst a base-born slave
  Who will desert the board to-night?
    Fill with sparkling wine,
    Come bow at its shrine,
    By Nature designed
To shroud unwonten cares for the grave.

The woes of life are bitter, my friends,
  Thickly they are falling 'round us,
And as we mark the uncertain ends
  The darkness still confounds us;
    A surcease from horror,
    A solace for sorrow,
    Joy without a morrow,
Where souls are happy mindless of ends.

Who will upbraid us for seeking repose
  From torrents of care brooding within?
Why sharpen each conscience to disclose
  The filthy depths of human sin?
    Let 's bury ev'ry grief,
    Sink our sorrows beneath,
    This life is too brief
To shadow one moment of time with woes.

Then fill up the bowl, boys, laugh and be gay,
  Nor count your sorrows ere they come,
Ye must gather sweet flowers in May
  Before they wither and are gone;
    Gaily quaff the cup, boys,
    Mingle the wine and joys,
    Life's cares are all but toys,
Let 's rejoice and be merry in our day.

MAN ALONE OF ANIMAL KIND.

Man alone of animal kind,
Who boasts the heritage of a mind,
Must chain his immortal reason
Or be damned by church for treason,
Be tethered to the blindest faith,
A criminal to stinking death ;
Ev'ry draught from priest, smile or frown,
Must close his eyes and gulp it down,
Nor ask to see the nauseous potion
Lest, seeing, he should change his notion,
So jealous are the gods of faith,
To doubt a priest's eternal death.
Is mind to such low depths sinking
That priests alone do the thinking,
Or is faith of such tender parts
That reason spoils its little tarts?
    O, reasoning man, awake, awake!
The iron chains of slav'ry break !
Kings nor priests were made to rule,
Save those the weak and these the fool ;
Where Nature has bequeathed a mind,
For nobler purpose 't is designed
Than bow forc'er a cringing slave
Or sleep within a hermit's cave.
What for your eyes, unless to look
Where Nature opes her spacious book !
And when ye turn its ample pages
Read from the folded leaf of ages,
Wherever thought can have a birth,
Read from the heavens and the earth,

From nature passed, where crumbling graves
Are silent records of its slaves.
Expand your thoughts and let them ride
Beyond old ocean's stormy tide,
Beyond the heaven's ethereal blue
Where circling worlds ne'er come to view;
Then say shall man humble his pride
And human reason be denied, .
As if ye were but thoughtless beast
To drag the plow for cunning priest!
Have mitred heads all wisdom found,
And are ye but playing the clown?
When God gives truth to his creatures,
Speaks he only through the preachers?
Go, ye priests, go teach your schools,
Frighten the weak, alarm the fools,
With fiery hells and stinking graves!
Go fatten on your cringing slaves!
Liberty, Liberty, still has a care,
And reason hears the human prayer,
Still hears the wailing and the groan
When wretched knaves enslave its own.
Men and women who should be free,
Bound to a craft and slavery,
With neither courage or control
To break the chains or free the soul,
Afraid of reason, afraid to think,
Lest light come in and they should sink,
They bow around the priestly caves
And lick the hands that made them slaves,

THE DEVIL SET HIS TRAPS ONE DAY.

The Devil set his traps one day
  To try the human fate,
And all who came within the way
  Were tempted by the bait;

And, strange to say, what curious bait
  He placed within each trap,
For some would pass in loathing hate
  What others straightway snap;

For he trapped lawyers and preachers,
  And game of many caste;
The Devil knows well all creatures,
  In each varying taste.

The women too all smiling came
  Into the monster's claws,
For some fashion tempted to shame
  With its little gewgaws.

Ev'ry one had his tender part
  The fiend could well detect,
In some 't was weakness of the heart,
  In some of intellect.

Some were entrapped with diadems,
  And some with plated brass,
Some only trapped with diamond gems,
  And some with colored glass.

But money was his powerful bait,
  How the fiend did shake it!
Though oft he had to swell its weight
  Ere the great would take it.

The rich and great the poor deride,
   To see them pennies take,
But e'en themselves a-quick decide
   When thousands are at stake.

Some, who resisted gold and fame,
   By wine were tempted sore,
And some, who knew no other shame,
   To woman's wiles gave o'er.

Much it amused his fiendship's heart,
   Patiently he waited,
Some only trapped by cunning art,
   Some caught e'en unbaited.

Now, as the Devil bagged his game,
   The fiend was heard to say,
Each man's his price, and 'll take the same
   If baited the right way.

OH, THOU ART BEAUTIFUL, MY LOVE!

Oh! thou art beautiful, my love,
   As the lilies are fair,
     When the dewy sweets,
     From silken leaflets,
   Perfume the balmy air.

Thy eyes are like the radiant stars
   In the argent field above,
     But softer each light,
     Twinkling bright,
   That fills my heart with love.

Thy hair is like the yellow rays
From setting sun unrolled,
Those locks of light
That drape the night
And paint the west with gold.

Thy breasts are like the drifted snow,
With gentle waves between,
As soft, as white,
As pearly quite,
But not so cold I ween.

Thy form is like an angel's form,
Flitting through heavenly air,
Tho' flesh and blood,
As pure as good,
As chaste and ever as fair.

Gladly I'd hie with thee away
To some more genial sky;
On beds of roses,
Where pleasure reposes,
We would dream of bliss for aye.

OLD PITMAN'S CHURCH.

Where Pitman's creek rolls through the wood,
And Pinch'em's road crosses its flood,
Within the century past there stood
Old Pitman's church;
Deep in its avenue of graves,
'Mid woods and cliffs and dingy caves
On ev'ry perch.

'T was here the pious herds convened,
From Satan's wrath and fury screened,
And matrons old and babes unweaned
    Were doubly blessed ;
For here, heaped in each sacred mound,
From life's grim cares and woes unbound,
    Their bodies rest.

As years rolled by in quick'ning flight
A change came o'er this hallow'd site,
And visions strange loomed up at night
    Among its graves ;
The weary traveler, delayed,
Saw ghostly forms grope thro' its glade
    Or out its caves.

One darksome night, wintry and cold,
A rustic lad strayed by the fold ;
The church was lit, as used of old,
    With sickly glare,
And all the dead in shrouds profuse
Were seated in the broken pews
    Or bowed in prayer.

Within the pulpit and alone,
Turning the pages one by one
As he was wont in years now gone
    A text to find,
The Parson stood in winding sheet,
His hair as white as snowy sleet
    In winter's time.

A gloomy form, ghastly in death,
Long bony hands, unearthly breath,
His shroud moldy with damp of earth
    And grave decays,

And all the dead sat grouped 'round
As listening to his solemn sound
     In other days.

The Parson prayed and then he preached,
A weird sound it was, and screeched
As when the midnight winds have reached
     Their dismal caves,
Then ev'ry ghost joined in the tones,
In hollow wails like sobbing groans
     Over their graves.

The songs were hushed, the service ended,
Forth the Parson's arms extended,
While in his voice strangely blended
     Pathos and fright,
Up rose the denizens of the graves
With muffled sound as when dark waves
     O'erflood the night.

" O Lord," he said, " we grow weary,
The grave is dark, its vaults dreary,
Ne'er a thought or vision cheery
     Within the the tomb,
Waiting Thy pleasure and command,
How long, how long until again
     Thou 'lt light this gloom ? "

A noise as when the waters move
Or black'ning storm rides high above,
And all was silent in the grove
     And dark its caves,
The dead, all dressed in their grave shrouds,
Rustled by like vapory clouds
     Back to their graves.

THE CLANDESTINE MEETING.

The night had drawn its vail above
   And bright the moon was shining,
We met within the cherry grove
   'Mid sweet flowers entwining,

Where balmy spring with gentle breeze,
   Where enchanted scenes delight,
Where music swells from all the trees
   And floats away on the night.

Softer than the moonlight above
   Kissing the fragrant flowers,
Two gentle hearts melting with love
   Were dreaming in its bowers ;

How oft I pressed her to my heart,
   Nestling closely to my breast,
We swore that we would never part,
   And mutual love confessed.

The hours passed in fond embraces,
   Joyous hours and bright,
A thousand vows, a thousand kisses,
   Quick winged the fleeting night.

But hark ! a sound disturbs our sweet,
   It comes thund'ring on the gale,
Her dad has found out our retreat,
   His big bull-dog's on the trail.

'T was a race for life, a wild, wild race,
   Sweet kisses little avail,
One might flee and angels embrace
   When a bull-dog's on his trail.

But to my legs, the best defense
'Gainst dad's bull or witches—
But ere I cleared the orchard fence
He had me by the breeches;

Add woe to grief, already sore
With my last leap in the air,
A charge of bird-shot sprinkled o'er
What the dog lately left bare.

Now all who read this tale of mine,
Who have clandestines incog.,
Though sweet the wooing by moonshine,
Look out for dad and his dog.

VALEDICTORY TO LOUISVILLE MEDICAL COLLEGE.

Adieu, my friends, a fond adieu!
The fates that break friendship's ties
Swell from the heart sorrowing tears
To stream from weeping eyes;
There's not a cord that binds the heart
But that's doomed to be broken,
There's not a meeting here on earth
But farewells must be spoken.

By the noblest science on earth,
Children of light, true in heart,
Bound by a friendship paternal,
E'en we, alas! too must part;
But parting, we'll pledge each other,
By the memory of the year,

To hold in mind ev'ry brother
  To truth and our science dear.

As time rolls on men become gods
  In knowledge and in power,
Chain the elements to control
  And ride the fleeting hour;
So, friends, search for the talisman,
  Throughout Nature's dusky haunt,
That opes the dark house of death
  And bids its powers avaunt!

Ye are armed, my friends, to combat
  The powers of sin and woe;
Ignorance and superstition
  Are manhood's greatest foe,
Let science's refulgent rays
  Illume all the dusky caves
Where mankind are chained in darkness
  Like dead men in their graves.

Fear not, my friends, the threat'ning cant
  When the wicked craftsmen frown,
Who among dusky clouds alone
  Seek their power and renown,
Carry the torch of truth boldly
  In the halls of gloomy night
Where mortal men in dungeons dark
  Are groping for the light.

This world is one vast battle-field,
  Strewn with its victims gory,
Whereon ye must contend for truth
  Tho' others reap all the glory;
Ye are the guardians of truth,
  'Tis yours to defend the right,

Let not your arms weaken their blows
When ye should strike with might.

Should we meet no more fraternally,
Mid life's passions wild and ruth,
E'er remember humanity's cry
And battle stoutly for truth;
Whatever is in store for men,
Let cunning priest call 't treason,
Nature's God is sacred still
To ev'ry son of reason.

Fear not fanaticism's scourge,
Nor e'er let your courage stay,
The martyrs of the dusky past
Are the heroes of to-day;
Ev'ry right of conscience and truth
Has fierce onslaught withstood,
And Liberty through gory fields
Been traced in tracks of blood.

Adieu, my friends, a last adieu!
The warmest love of my heart
Ever swells in kindness for you,
Regretting that we must part;
When on the rough desert of time
I am faint with weary strife,
I'll e'er remember our companionship,
Fair oases in my life.

THE DYING INFIDEL.

He's dying now! how dark the shadows dwell
Upon his brow! no beacon light, no ray
Of hope to illume the dusky pall of death,
Black as night it draws it murky folds round
His last couch.   Life to him was a flickering dream,
An aimless and ambitionless shadow—
The past a dreary, senseless delusion,
The present a fleeting dream, the future
Black with woeful uncertainty ;
But he's dying now, let cold charity
Mantle him from fanaticism's gaze.
Insult not the dead ; fanaticism's deaf
To the reasons that shaped his thought
Or darkened his soul; his hopes, his fears, his all,
Lie smoldering in the spark that yet warms
His weakening heart.   Deal gently with his frailties.
Death, the dusky monster of human woe,
On black pinions hovers 'mid murky clouds
Like a shadow o'er him, waiting fiend-like
To escort his wretched soul through the
Gloomy corridors of eternity.   He's dying now ;
The gentle wooings of Revelation,
The kind admonitions of faith and hope
Are strangers to him ; all around
Is as black as midnight's darkest storm.
Like a sinking ship on a tempestuous sea,
When the surging waves are black with the
Spectral clouds of night—engulfed the craft—
So down into the turbulent waters of human sorrow,
Driven from rock to rock, from billow to billow,
By the fierce waves that surge the moral soul,
Lost in the fog of human reason, he sinks

In the grave his aimless ambition digged.
Oh! let us not upbraid him as a fiend
Because he is dying an infidel,
But o'er his cold, helpless grave strew the flowers
Of human love and Christian kindness,
Commending his soul to God, who purposed
Its being. Was he a fanatic! What strange dreams
Infatuated his wild, weird fancies
And stalked like ghost through his frenzied slumber
Is not for us to know or even to surmise.
Was he a kind husband, a loving father,
A warm friend? Had he never a noble emotion
That might be told in extenuation
Of the most awful crime of unbelief?
Is it retribution! Are they demons
That glare wildly upon his dying couch
And craze his soul with shadowy presence?
Is it remorse that torments his soul
And makes his dying so terrible? Why does
He foam in the death struggle like a madman
Tearing the gratings of his cell to escape?
Is his soul in anguish wrestling to free
Itself from the wild fiends that torture it,
Or is't all but a strange human fancy,
But a weird vision of our own
Imagining? Is he really suffering;
Are we not drawing upon our fancies
For shrouds to drape the enemies of our faith?
Realize the dying moral anguish
In the deep and unconscious sleep of death!
Is it not nature convulsed yet thoughtful,
Under a kind anesthesia, tearing the
Dreamless soul from its senseless body,
Where life, ever jealous of its tenure,

Struggles e'en in the very jaws of death
To reclaim its own ?   How oft I have marked
The gesticulations of the dying
As deepens the coma that slumbers into death,
The wild-glaring expression of anguish,
The gentle smile of tenderest affection,
The fierce contortions of the body,
The low and muttering delirium,
Sometimes solemn, sometimes farcical,
The delusions of sight, the grasping out
At invisible specters in the air !
All construed by the friends of the dying,
Who 've lingered to catch the last gurgling groan
Frothed through the flaccid lips of death
In ominous rattle, as best might suit
Their anticipations of the finale :
Sweet heavenly visions, dire strains of hell,
Woven by a thousand cunning creeds
To suit their own respective hopes and fears
And forever damn and blacken their enemies.

THE RACE FOR WEALTH.

The race for wealth is madd'ning fast,
    In ev'ry land appears
The Shylocks of human blood
    Feasting on human tears ;

The rich are proud, the poor oppressed,
    And money is our king,
E'en Liberty bows with drooping head
    Before its sordid ring ;

Millionaires, princes, railroad lords,
   Bond-holders puffed with bloat,
Hold the reins of state and commerce,
   Hold Congress and its vote;

Only the poor, the wretched poor,
   Who live by humble toils,
Are still oppressed by state and church,
   Are still used for the spoils.

Oh! to be poor, and have it said
   'T is meanness of the blood,
Who dress in silks and satins rare
   Are of a nobler brood.

'T is wealth, 't is wealth in madd'ning craze,
   Society has to blame,
Ferments all wars, plots all crimes,
   Fills earth with woe and shame.

For gold men swim thro' lake of blood
   And die on battle field,
Or ironclads plow ev'ry sea,
   Bristling with murd'rous steel.

This craze for wealth, this selfish strife,
   Leads through ev'ry nation,
Even Christians call it progress
   And civilization.

A VISION.

The day had hushed its busy sound,
The night had drawn its curtains round,
Beside Buckhorn I sat me down
    To muse alone,
And in the darkness all profound
    I heard a groan.

The shades of night then piercing through,
The strangest form came to my view,
Of its cloven feet, its barbed tail,
    I scarce can tell,
Its curious horns, its coat of mail,
    And sulphur smell.

As I yet gazed in horrid fright,
I had almost taken to flight,
When said the specter, " I'm the Devil ;
    No harm is meant ;
I would not use friends uncivil,
    Now be content."

Still, as I almost quaked for fear,
In confidence Satan drew near ;
So bland his smiles, I thought no ill
    Could e'er be meant,
And then he praised old Campbellsville
    To some extent.

Softly he spoke : " Thou mayst not know it,
My secret do thou not blow it,
To me is given the reins of state,
    A task I love,
To shape the lives of all I love
    On earth above;

" But strange rumors have come below,
The truth of which I want to know,
My imps have all taken to flight ;
    And well they should,
If this be truth that's come to light
    'Bout J.......

" Despite of hell and all my hate,
    J.....'s determined to be great ;

As pots with brass and mules with cheek
  Were made or born,
All glory hangs o'er Brushy Creek,
  Famed Rubicon."

Said I, " My friend, why such a fright?
Give J.. a lift, he'll treat thee right."
Quoth he, " What needs this man of lift,
  Champion brave,
Whose politic fame already 's reft
  All hell conclave?

" Like the rolling of an earthquake,
When dusky columns of night break,
Subjects infernal howl and shake
  In dread and awe,
As all the nation 's rushed to make
  J. . . . Governor!

" In hell I heard of his great fame,
And straight I rose from sulphur and flame
This Cæsar's ambition to cool,
  Lest he, o'ergrown,
And not content with earthly rule,
  Attack my throne.

" Many the restless hours I spent,
But I've seen J. . . . and am content;
If guts were brains, and brass was power
  To overwhelm,
I'd abnegate this very hour
  My infernal realm."

What's in Fate's store may not be told,
Nor how much gas some men can hold,
Puffed like bladders with wind and roar
  And pride disgusting,

But if J. . . . swells a little more
  There'll be some bu'sting.

"But," quoth the Devil, "I must be going;
This little conference be not blowing,
Lest wicked malice should enjoy
  My raid to-night;
Next time I come for J. . . ., boy,
  'T won't be from fright."

And then he raised him on his shanks
And cut a jig in fiendish pranks,
And last he said, with cunning smile
  Softening its bane,
"I'll see you, friend, some other while—
  We'll meet again."

HE WANTS TO BE GOVERNOR.

Our J. . . . ., of Brushy Creek,
  Although a little raw,
Has all the brass and all the cheek
  To make a Governor.
Good luck's better'n silver or gold,
  Greatness a child of Fate,
One ass counseled a prophet of old,
  Another may counsel the State;
When the lightnings smite those who'd rule,
  Its reddest bolts are pliant,
Just as likely to strike a mule
  As 't is to strike a giant.
Take courage, J. . . ., from what I've said,
  And trust to luck for aye,
The asses survive tho' the prophets 're dead,
  And the fools will never die.

THE STOLEN KISS.

I stole a kiss from my sweetheart one day,
 As we walked along the lane,
She asked me if, like a cowardly thief,
 I'd ne'er return it again.

Only a criminal caught in the act,
 Where justice commands so bold,
I made haste to amend the wrong I'd done,
 And paid it all back tenfold.

But somehow I thought so terrible crime
 Unrevenged should never go,
At least some penance I thought to exact,
 And gave her a hundred more.

I told her if she'd forgive me this time
 I'd ne'er again act amiss;
She forgave as only a woman can,
 And we sealed it with a kiss.

THE FATHER IS GROWING FEEBLER.

The father is growing feebler,
 The mother's getting gray,
With tottering steps and infirm
 They tread life's downward way;
One foot upon the slippery sod
 And one within the grave,
They are not what they used to be
 When they were young and brave.

Their minds are weak'ning like their limbs,
 And tott'ring down the hill,

But though they 've grown old and feeble,
　We 'll ever love them still;
The mother's becoming childish,
　But she shall bear no blame,
Though she should tread upon our toes,
　We 've tread on hers the same.

The endearing joys of childhood
　Are still to mem'ry sweet,
As kindly our parents watched us,
　Our little tott'ring feet,
And when our limbs were so feeble
　We scarce could walk alone
They led us gently by the hand
　Till we were older grown;

So now they may lean upon us,
　As they 've been parents true,
As they have helped our tender years
　We 'll give them honor due;
And down the steeper plane of life,
　As near the other shore,
Our stronger limbs will bear them up,
　God pass them gently o'er.

When we too shall be older grown
　And totter on life's brink,
May our children buoy us up
　Lest we untimely sink;
Kindly remember the children,
　Nor is our kindness vain,
When we are old and enfeebled
　They 'll remember us again.

AND YOU WOULD ASK, MY DEAREST FRIEND.

And you would ask, my dearest friend,
  With feelings all sedate,
What I think of life's final end
  And of our future state?

And yet you know it is the rule,
  In every land agreed,
To call him knave, or at least fool,
  Who dares dispute the creed.

The jaundiced man sees thro' his bile
  Only yellow minions,
So hard for men to reconcile
  Diff'rence of opinions.

And since, my friend, you so desire
  To hear my humble view,
All hopes and fears mankind inspire,
  Whether they're false or true:

We are frail creatures of the sods,
  And so I'd have us taken,
Of all the creeds and all the gods,
  Some surely are mistaken;

And yet one hope to mortals given
  Let's leave the human race,
May all mankind get to heaven,
  If there be such a place;

But as to hell's dark, gloomy goal,
  Be't never God's disgrace,
Digged by priest to extort toll
  Off of the human race.

To know a thing by faith's record
Will feed the simple mind,
But stronger minds need stronger food,
And faith you know is blind.

To sum up all that can be said,
We know not whence it came,
And when we look beyond the dead
'T is darkness all the same;

Although the hopes of mortal men
Can surely nothing prove,
Whatever be man's final end
We hope for peace and love;

At least we would not fright man's hope
With 'maginary fears,
If heaven's gate we may not ope,
We'd dry all human tears.

THE CULPRIT.

Why from this lonesome cell,
Like a Devil incarnate,
Look I thro' this iron grate
As from the jaws of hell?

Am I human beast or fiend,
That from this damp gloom
As from a living tomb
I gaze these bars between?

What crime 'gainst human right,
That dark dungeons close

Their massive iron doors ﹀
In perpetual night?

Ye who walk the streets, brave
    In liberty's broad ways,
    Count not the weary days
Dragging me to the grave;

Mark the mischief that's done
    In Justice's name each day,
    Human beings waste 'way,
Shut out from air and sun;

Then your proud hearts would melt,
    E'en if they were of stone,
    To hear each piteous groan
And feel what we have felt.

Dark dungeons fettering the soul
    And binding men enslaved,
    Knelled, coffined, and graved,
Dragging wearily to their goal.

Human torture will be brief;
    Death, no better friend or truer,
    When hearts can no more endure,
Comes hap'ly to man's relief.

'TIS A GLORIOUS PRIVILEGE, MY FRIEND.

'Tis a glorious privilege, my friend,
That virtuous minds the right defend,
When to a heart by guile betrayed,
Revenge is sweet e'en to a maid;

A dreary life, weary and forlorn,
With never a rose except the thorn,
With nothing left that it might trace
For womanhood except disgrace.

Why should I hide my face in shame,
When he, who stole my virtuous name
With honeyed words of vile deceit,
Unbranded walks through ev'ry street?
Oh! must I seek a cloistered den,
Secluded from the gaze of men,
From society's smile forever barred,
He proud with conscience still unscarred?

The tend'rest heart, estranged by guile,
Is deceived by the villain's smile,
So well the villain plays his part,
So confiding a woman's heart;
She scorns to impute a motive small
In him to whom she trusts her all,
Till she wakes from her dreams dismayed
To find her heart and soul betrayed.

Think ye not, when love's been slighted,
Vengeance can sleep unrequited!
Where disgrace is added to slight,
Hatred adds to vengeance might;
Honeyed words, now bitter as gall,
Sting the heart they did enthrall,
And round it draw in circling fire
The terrors of revengeful ire.

Yes, I will haunt him day and night,
No night too dark, no day too bright,
I'll dog his steps from street to street,
I'll hunt him down for vengeance sweet;

No more shall peace e'er be his boast,
He's my murderer, I'm his ghost,
I'll shadow him like a spirit lost,
He yet shall learn of virtue's cost;

Nor think, my friends, that with this life
Shall end the horrors of our strife,
His dying couch I'll overwhelm,
Follow his manes to darker realm;
In the land of shades, dead man's clime,
I'll hunt his spirit with its crime,
Along the shadowy coasts of hell
Sweet vengeance'll follow it still.

Though the world scorns a woman's bane,
It feasts the author of her shame,
While she must die to hide her face,
He's left to boast of his disgrace;
The voice that dooms her folly blind
But welcomes him to other crime,
She is the wench, hers is the woe,
He is still society's beau.

O, women with confiding heart,
Ye who have never felt its smart,
Ye who have found your lovers true
And trusted them in honor due,
Pity ye not my sorrowing groan?
E'en my fate might have been your own,
Had they on whom your love was thrust
Proven recreant to the trust.

THERE IS A SLEEP, A LONG, LONG SLEEP.

There is a sleep, a long, long sleep,
    When to the grave we take us,
No more to tell its mystic dreams
    Shall mortal man awake us;

For over the dreams of that couch
    Death hangs its drap'ry of night,
A dusky cloud all black'ning dire
    Before the human sight.

Dark are the gloomy halls of night
    Wherein this couch is spread,
The specters of another sphere
    Guard round its sleeping dead;

Profound the slumber that they sleep,
    Unknown their names or day,
Eternity's silent witnesses
    Still sleeping on for aye.

ONE WORLD AT A TIME.

One world at a time's enough of strife,
    Where passion overwhelms,
Virtue's a child of real life
    And not of shadowy realms;
They may howl who are wont to claim
    Virtue's an heir of faith,
Credulity the magic sesame
    That opes the gates of death.

Live for the life open to view,
　The wrongs of the weak redress,
To country and to humanity true—
　Angels are not in distress;
They may rant who speak of a birth
　Beyond the cloudy sky,
Heaven'd bloom with flowers on earth
　If oppression's tears were dry.

Dream not visions of golden strand
　Where white-robed angels tread,
Death hangs its shroud o'er hopes of man,
　The poor are begging bread;
Awake, ye dreamers, awake, awake!
　Who sleep among life's graves,
Let clouds drift on and wild winds break,
　Earth has work for its slaves.

Why craze the soul with vapory fears,
　The heart with sad misgiving,
Man drifts on an ocean of tears
　'Mid wrecks of the living;
Go feed the poor, the sick attend,
　Go succor human needs,
The God Almighty needs no friend,
　Humanity only bleeds.

THE AMERICAN SLAVE.

Ye have been slaves, too true indeed,
Mere bondsmen, an ignoble breed,
E'en 's the dull ass that plows the corn,
But to no higher honors born,

And this too where Liberty's face
Blushes not at its own disgrace;
Yet ye're human and have a soul
That will survive when earth is old,
When mountain from mountain's riven
By dissolving blasts of heaven.
Oh! think ye that there are no tears
Falling from Mercy on our cares?
Oh! think ye not the wretched slave,
Bound by tyrants on Freedom's grave,
Has ne'er a groan to pierce the skies
Or gush the tears in Mercy's eyes?
The time will come, thro' nature wide
No trace is left of human pride,
Shorn of its glory, in decay
Human grandeur passes away!
Who then can boast of wealth or birth—
The true metewand is moral worth;
Color will fade like dusky night
Before the day's advancing light,
But if the heart in ev'ry grace
Is to be shown within the face,
What strange contrasts will greet the sight!
Some fair as morn, some black as night,
And here and there a deeper stain
The blackest night would pale with shame.

APOSTROPHE TO DEATH.

Cold and dark is thy form, O Death!
And icy is thy vapory breath,
Black are the dismal chambers
Wherein thy unwilling slaves are chained,

What eye e'er pierced thy shadowy spheres
Or ear heard whisperings from thy realms?
As ghostly as the night thy visions,
As hollow as the midnight voices
Thy echoes, as silent as eternal
Are all thy legions, O Death!
Though one by one our friends and loved ones
Are wrapt in thine iron embrace,
Thy arms unrelenting as thy silence,
And thy embrace as cold as eternal.

POETRY.

What is Poetry but polished thoughts
    In euphonic language dressed,
Striking our ears in mellow notes
    With concurrent ideas expressed;
Hearts and souls that think and feel,
    'T is the language of feeling,
It lights the mind with sunbeams   .
    Where shadows were concealing
Passions that long'd to break the spell
That chain'd them in life's gloomy cell.

Is this world all dark and friendless?
    Hope environs its despair;
Is there a storm on life's horizon
    Lurid with its lightning glare,
Where crushing thunders peal in tones
    Like the tolling of a knell?
Bright sunbeams hide behind each cloud,
    Smiling 'bove the surging swell,
Though discord 'larms the fright'ned ear,
Hope stays its grief and stills its fear.

Is life's fancy serene and sweet,
  Hope undim'd by Sorrow's tear,
With radiant sun-refulgent sphere
  Warming, bright'ning ev'ry care?
Birds sing sweet on every bower,
  Sunbeams gild the passing hour,
Sweetest perfume from scented flower
  Lends charm to nature's power,
Gladdening the heart with hopes given
Like sweetest visions of heaven.

Such is Poesy, music of Nature,
  Thrilled on the chords of the heart,
'Mid the lights and shadows of life
  Where mankind enacts his part;
Life's bright with joy, or dark with woe,
  As the heart's bright or dark within,
As the soul's buoyed up with hope
  Or blackened with fear and sin,
The outward life in its broad design
Portrays the inward soul and mind.

DOUBTS.

The darkest page in human sorrow,
  The saddest tale of human woes,
Gloomy nights of uncertain morrow,
  Shadowy, vague and mystic foes,
Is it well for those who dream
  That far beyond the murky night
They can catch a hallowed gleam
  From a land of radiance bright?

Faith warms up the chilly waters
  And calms life's ever-raging groan,
For with the peace such hope flatters
  We launch into the great unknown;
As the dark clouds gather round us,
  And death's cold waters roll beneath,
Reason and learning confound us,
  No light but the dim light of faith.

If the grave's Faith's funeral knell,
  Vapory as the fleeting breath,
Still there's magic in its spell
  To soothe the wild terrors of death,
Though from the land of gloomy shade
  No wand'ring voice has e'er returned,
And gloomy doubt in night dismayed
  Weeps o'er the prospects of its morn.

But oh! what a wild, wretched thought,
  The saddest thought of all our dreams,
That we are here only to rot,
  Our life's but the shadow it seems!
Hope, brightest boon to man given,
  The golden link in life's frail chain,
Tethers the dull soul to heaven,
  A panacea for ev'ry bane.

THE SUICIDE'S SOLILOQUY.

Tired of life, tired of life,
  Without one ray of light,
A never-ceasing struggling strife
  From morn till weary night.
Oh! what is death that I should fear
His vap'ry breath or scalding tear,

Shall I forego every strife
And live to woe for sake of life?

Dark and rayless the dusky sky
  That clouds my moral sun,
'T is not madness that seeks to die,
  'T is sweet oblivion;
If torturing fate prolong my doom,
Shall I wait for it to come,
Or supplement with the knife
The discontent of weary life?

What charm has this earth to bind me
  Till woes their plans mature,
Madden, torture, and confine me
  Long 's nature will endure?
Nature is slow, torture 's severe,
I pray to go but still I 'm here,
Misery wrecked 'mid surging strife,
With no respect for soul or life.

They tell me in the dread beyond   .
  I 'll find a darker life,
That sorrow knows no deeper wound
  Than its infernal strife;
Ye wretched shades avaunt, depart,
Ye have dismayed my trembling heart;
The blow 's given, and who can tell
Is it heaven or is it hell?

This draught 's sweet Oblivion's steep,
  I know 't is death to sip,
He who would sleep the long, long sleep,
  May press it to his lip;
Who would not die? Terrors in wrath
Avenging lie around my path.
O sweet repose, I welcome thee!
From life's grim foes at least I 'm free.

A FRAGMENT.

What can be said to soothe a mother's pain,
What sophistry ease her infernal bane,
When, like a dagger rusting in her heart,
A mad fiend tears the aching wound apart,
When her unwedded child with down-cast face
Is forced at last to reveal her disgrace,
Bring forth a babe, where slanderous tongues are rife,
A young mother before she is a wife?
Heaven, methinkst thou hast a soothing tear
To weep over a child's untimely bier,
But no tear can erase so foul a stain
Nor balm distill to soothe a mother's pain;
Society, 't is by thy artificial blame
Woman alone must bear the lash of shame.
Heaven, methinkst, still loves the ruined maid
As well as him by whom she is betrayed.
But, fond mother, this can never still thy grief,
Retribution brings the heart no relief;
Far better death, O child of foul embrace,
Than hope smothered in eternal disgrace!

THE DYING MOSLEM.

They tell me that I'm dying,
  That I'm passing fast away,
The night of death is creeping
  O'er scenes of time and day,
And my soul must take its flight
  In the great eternity.

How softly fall the shadows
  As they gather round my bed,

The air is filled with music,
  Good genii lightly tread,
If this indeed be dying,
  Sweet the chambers of the dead.

Do not weep for me, loved ones,
  Do not let your hearts grieve you,
Though 't is sorrow to my soul
  Thus sadly to bereave you,
To me the parting's Paradise,
  And death only to leave you.

From celestial shores streaming
  Thro' the dusky vail of night,
Darker grows the gloom of death,
  Clearer the heavens bright,
The angels are waiting for me,
  Hovering on wings of light.

Oh! where is the grim Eblis,
  Who so oft 'larms the dying?
Keen pains of dissolution
  Through ev'ry nerve are flying,
But death's no fear for the soul
  On hope and faith relying.

Though my ears are growing dull
  And my eyes are getting dim,
I can catch from other spheres
  The angels' joyous hymn,
Its echoes of soft music
  'Tire my soul with vim.

Why talk to me of living,
  As if death had alarms!
Why talk to me of dying,
  As if life still had charms!

23

Oh! talk to me of Paradise,
  Reposing in angel arms!

Come place thy hand on my brow,
  The death-damp's gathering there,
Come kneel close beside my bed,
  Together we'll offer prayer
That we yet may meet again,
  And no more parting there.

Bury me quietly away,
  Free from slander's wicked shaft,
There let impious men mock me,
  Skeptics and atheists laugh;
Resting sweetly in Islam,
  There's no nobler epitaph.

O, ye men who boast learning
  Where science binds its fair wreath,
Why attempt to break the charm,
  The Koran's bright hope and faith?
Why dash the sweet cup of life
  From the trembling lips of death?

EPITAPH ON A DOCTOR.

Here he lies, shorn of his breath
By the ruthless hand of Death;
How strange 't is that thus he ends,
Since he and Death were such friends!
Who hence will expect protection
From professional connection?

EPITAPH ON A LAWYER.

Here he lies, a lawyer still,
  Demurring for sake of cavil,
He mortgaged his soul for gain,
  Let him enjoin the devil;
Perhaps limitation 'll save him
  Like poor insolvent paupers;
If not, he yet may appeal
  To writ of habeas corpus,
Or file bills of exceptions,
  Rejoinder or cross-petition,
Thus still to delay action
  And defraud perdition.

EPITAPH ON A SOUR SAINT.

Here lies a man whose sour face
Was his only stock in grace;
No other excellence given,
He frowned himself into heaven.

RECONCILIATION.

Let us speak no more of sections
  That lead us to bitter strife,
But renew the love again
  That bound our earlier life;
As we are a union of States,
  Let us bind together in heart,

And forever heal the wounds
  Our passions tore apart.

No North, South, East, nor West
  For jealous malice to roam,
But a nation of brothers
  In Freedom's proudest home;
Let us forget the bloody strife
  As we've buried away its braves,
May we ne'er tear their wounds
  Nor open their graves.

When we teach our children
  Our country's common fates,
May we ever speak softly
  Of the war between the States;
Tho' the battle joined fiercely
  And the friends of thousands bled,
Let us bury all the past
  In the grave with its dead.

As to the wounds of foes,
  They are made with poisoned steel,
They are like running sores,
  They may scab but never heal;
Then in forbearance be gentle,
  And this maxim ever heed,
E'en the wounds of brothers
  May open and may bleed.

Tho' many a widowed heart
  Has sorrowed out its pain,
Whose husband and child
  Have been mingled with the slain,
From New England's frozen shore
  To Florida's coral reef

Homes have been made desolate
And hearts filled with grief.

There are some pangs in memory
That linger with us yet,
And tho' we have forgiven all
We never may forget;
Let our lips be sealed in silence,
Nor to posterity restore them,
But bear our secrets to the grave
That they may never know them.

Then dwell no more on passions
That filled the land with mourning,
But look to the future unborn
For its brighter dawning;
May God bless our country,
Shield it from evil fates,
And give us a union of hearts
In this union of States.

THE OLD MAIDS' JOLLY CLUB.

BY MARY ANN.

Around their snuff they sit and chat,
Now talk of this, and then of that;
Like lawyers astute great questions handle,
Either in fashion or in scandal,
Such topics great they do sledge on
As society, state, and religion.
With huge mashed swabs and gobs of spit,
Tobacco juice and vulgar wit,
Each knowing one but nods and winks,
And straight she speaks just that she thinks.

They talk of minds that are distracted,
Of meetings soon to be protracted,
Of those who ought to be converted,
Of wives and children long deserted,
Of crusades on the liquor shops,
Of failures in the baby crops,
All society and its construction,
The last wedding and seduction.
They tell of girls, with pretty faces,
Yielding to wealth their natural graces;
How priests, tempt by wicked beauty,
Stray from the narrow path of duty,
How the old toper paints his nose,
How blooming widows sigh for beaux,
While some old maids, to damn the truth,
Curl and dye to resemble youth ;
How one who oft has gi'n the mitten
Finds beaux no longer to be smitten,
And one who flaunts about so proud
Nor deigns to smile on common crowd,
Dresses in silks and diamonds replete—
Her great grandsire cleaned the street.
They talk of some who o'er wash-tub
Strain their backs to scour and scrub,
Still priding on a family fame,
Boasting the heritage of name,
As if mere blood could make a race
Or save 't from poverty's disgrace.
'T is whispered, " Rosy, the high-fly gal,
Has gone for repair to the hospital ;
Thus folly oft' must fee the doctor
That brooks neither advice nor proctor.
She played long, played well her game,
But woe's hers who's caught in shame,

E'en though she should trust the preacher,
Human faith's an onerous feature ;
A wicked smile's a tempting bait,
She repents in vain who repents too late."
'T is thus the gossip floats around,
Each curious soul drinks in the sound,
As convivial lads in drunken roar,
Who drink and pass the cup for more.

REPLY TO MARY ANN.

BY AN OLD MAID.

Ah, Mary Ann, you are a case !
Think you to hide so fair a face,
And 'neath your feminine *nom de plume*
In male attire to yield the broom ?
Should the jackass to sing essay,
Think you the birds 'd mistake the bray ?
Did e'er yet the choristers hail
A cackling goose for a nightingale ?
Ah, Mary Ann, too thin, too thin,
There's too much beard upon your chin,
Too much mustache for Mary Ann,
Yet scarce enough to make a man,
Your feet too big, too frail your shanks,
To play on old maids your boyish pranks.
As you 'd laugh till your side stitches
To see a woman dressed in breeches,
With a spurred heel and a jockey hat,
Smoking a pipe like a regular flat,
Loafing around all the summer
And tipping the glass with ev'ry bummer,

Then why not smile at an old he-goat
Flouncing around in a petticoat,
Stuffed up with gas and airs uncommon,
To have the world think he's a woman?
Mary Ann, do not think uncivil,
Some respect's due e'en to the Devil,
But if you'd be poet or poetess,
Sing of the hoppers that hop in the grass,
The katydids and straddle bugs,
Of pills, of potions, of jars or jugs,
But beware when you attempt to rub
Your scabby back 'gainst the Old Maids' Club.
If perchance you're matrimonially inclined,
Dress like a man, come speak your mind,
But love 'll never smile at slander
Long's there's a goose to every gander.
If fool man would but stop his teasing,
Few maids would e'er repine for squeezing,
And such as died thus celibate,
Never expire cursing their fate.

MARY ANN'S REJOINDER.

My dear old maid, so amply fit
Are all thy lines as holy writ,
It seems as if some airy sprite
Had whispered words for you to write;
And e'en now thy chastening dart
Quivers deep in a lover's heart,
Who cares neither for crooks nor age,
But loves the wrinkles of the sage.
The simple boast their soft blue eyes
And azured cheeks like summer skies,

Mere transient glow of sunny hours
Lending gloss to withering flowers;
Our sage wisdom is forced to smile,
Such fleeting shadows o'er time's dial—
Let youthful vanity learn its cost,
Its lilies, nipped by early frost,
Droop their heads and die repining
O'er dark hours that once were shining;
But you and I, my sweet old maid,
Long from such frivolity 've strayed,
We 'ne no more tempt' by gaudy youth
From this vain world to hide the truth,
We'll quit our paint and cotton breast
And grow old in mutual cursedness.
False hair, false calves, and e'en the " bustle"
We'll throw from off each limb and muscle,
With striped hose and high-heeled shoes
No more our aching corns abuse,
Nor ribs tight round our livers bind
To improve on nature's design,
With laced corsets or other toys
Pressing abdominal avoirdupois;
We'll throw aside cosmetic graces,
We'll show the world our real faces,
Nor fill wrinkles with dirty mushes,
Nor paint 'em up to look like blushes;
We'll lay aside our porcelain teeth,
For snags of nature's own bequeath,
Take off our rings of plated brass
And little gewgaws of colored glass,
Lay them with our hopes and fears
On the grave of younger years,
And, kneeling by departed youth,
If't break our hearts, confess the truth

Engraven on nature's withered pages ;
We 'll lie no more about our ages,
Erase records from family Bible,
Nor 'cuse its dates of wicked libel.

THE OLD MAIDS' SONG.

We dear old maids sit in the shades,
   For lovers still we tarry,
Few are so old, with hearts so cold,
   That they despair to marry ;
Long shanks and lean, crusty and mean,
   Are bachelors full many,
We 'll find a mate if we but wait,
   There 's surplus not any.

With many pranks we hide our shanks,
   As daily they grow thinner,
With plaster still the wrinkles fill
   To please each crusty sinner ;
Tho' still by fate we 're doomed to wait,
   Our hopes will ne'er miscarry,
Some wrinkled "cus" as old as us
   Perchance 'll want to marry.

We 've still a tongue as good as young,
   Tho' long our cheeks 've faded,
Woman's weapon to depend upon
   As strong as when God made it ;
We 'll ne'er declare for matches rare,
   Nor will we choice be,
But we 'll take most any drake
   Who quacks to matrimony.

True, some old fool may break the rule,
  Marry a girl in her teen,
Or some widow get the bidder,
  And surely he's as green ;
But well you know we're due a beau,
  And for that beau we're prating,
And still we'll try ; if we should die,
  We can but die a-waiting.

EPITAPH ON A PET SQUIRREL.

Here lies poor Bun, free from toil and fun,
  Peace to his moldering sand,
He's made of life's sad wicked strife
  As much as many a man ;
When the tears of a hundred years
  Have flooded sorrow's rife,
Few moldering bones in the graveyard strown
  Will be better known in life ;
Such is fame, sad flickering flame
  Burning o'er ambitions rotten,
Time's circling flight closes in night,
  And all are soon forgotten.

THE HEIRESS.

I've a few thousand dollars,
  And nearly as many beaux,
Sometimes I think 's my money,
  Sometimes my pretty nose ;
They all say I'm a darling,
  A queenly beauty at any rate,

But then the boys will flatter
The girls of great estate.

There's Jane, the bonanza heiress,
The diff'rence makes me smile,
As homely as blue mud she,
Till her father struck "ile;"
Then the freckles faded fast,
Beauty did each blemish rout,
But never till she was rich
Could a lover find it out.

Then there's Kate, once very rich,
Beauty traced in ev'ry line,
Many a pimp bowed at her feet
At the bidding of her mind;
But "dad's ile" well ran dry,
Stocks decreased, the banks broke,
And then her mercenary beaux
Said it was all a joke.

Ah ladies, with great fortunes
And many beaux, beware!
'T is gold and not your princely selves,
Nor yet your raven hair;
Many a mercenary flatterer,
With heart as cold as stone,
Will take you for your fortunes,
Who'd scorn your hands alone.

Pure love is unostentatious,
Free from affectation's guile,
Where two hearts beat as one
And smile responds to smile;
In happy congeniality wed,
Sweet contentment rules supreme—

Wealth must come of honest toil
And not from Cupid's dream.

Would you stoop so low for gain,
When the night is dark and cold,
Steal into their sleeping chambers
And murder men for gold?
By the same pride of soul
Restrain your greed for pelf,
Nor smother an innocent heart
To squander its wealth.

IF NOBODY CALLS YOU A RASCAL.

If nobody calls you a rascal,
If nobody calls you a thief,
You've cut a small figure in life,
Your glory will be brief,
The chances are the poor-house
Will come to your relief;

If nobody calls you a scoundrel,
If nobody impeaches your truth,
You may have plowed potatoes
Without competition forsooth,
Aged you're a worthless crone,
And an imbecile in youth.

Never was there a profession,
Nor yet a business so sedate,
From clergyman to the bootblack,
Without the rivalry and hate
To which ungenerous competitions
In vile vituperations degenerate;

Never was glory so transcendent,
  Nor character so free from stain,
That some would not dare mock
  The eminence they could not attain,
And whom they could not emulate
  Would slander all the same.

But dare, friends, to do the right,
  Slanderous opinions none the less,
There's an iron will enemies respect
  And heaven will surely bless,
There's nothing in human worth
  Except 't is measured by success.

PATRICK HENRY'S ADDRESS.

Are we freemen or are we slaves,
Do we shudder o'er our graves,
Have we the heart that braves
    Death serenely?

Has life for us such mellow strains
It can soften the tyrant's chains,
It can soothe the infernal banes
    Of monarchy?

I know not what others may cherish,
But as for me, survive or perish,
Sink or swim, my heart's fond wish,
    Death or liberty.

Why talk of peace? there is no peace
Submitting to fouler disgrace,
The chains of tyrants never case
    Them willingly.

Already war sounds its discord,
Thunders at Lexington and Concord,
And gory streams a crimson flood
  From liberty.

Why stand we idle, must we yield?
Our bravest men are in the field,
Disgrace or liberty dyes the steel
  Of victory.

Ye who would be England's slaves,
To your homes as to your graves,
Ye sons of liberty, Freedom's braves,
  All rally!

Strike for your rights; may God inspire
Every heart with a noble desire;
On land, on sea, thro' blood or fire,
  Strike bravely!

DECEIT.

Who meets you with a fawning grace,
Who greets you with a smiling face,
Who talks to you of others' disgrace,
  Take care!
Many a smile so soft and sweet
Is but a cloak for vile deceit—
  Beware!

Many a suave and cunning device
Is fostered by a friendship nice,
Each deceitful villain has his price—
  Take care!

The evil genii never sleep,
So your jealous vigils keep—
        Beware!

Many to your face 'll defend you
Who behind your backs rend you;
Friends they are only to spend you—
        Take care!
Praise to-day, to-morrow abuse you,
Friends indeed while they may use you—
        Beware!

The cur licks with menial fawning,
He 'll bite you ere another morning,
His mouth is but a hell yawning—
        Take care!
There 's no danger that 's more complete
Than snares hidden beneath deceit—
        Beware!

A wretch of evil inclination
Wooes with flattering insinuation,
He courts you for a foul relation—
        Take care!
Be on your guard whene'er he pass,
Sure he 's a viper in the grass—
        Beware!

MY MOTHER-IN-LAW.

I was born in Taylor County
    Sometime before the war,
I married in Campbellsville,
    And I 've got a mother-in-law.

I can ride a Texas bull,
  I can climb a buzz-saw,
But God protect the country
  When I meet my mother-in-law.

I've seen the fossil mastodon
  And his stupendous jaw,
It made me weep to see it—
  So like my mother-in-law!

I've been among the Comanches,
  But never stood in awe
Before the face of man or beast
  Till I met my mother-in-law.

I've been in bloody battles,
  In the thickest of the war,
But a shell's a thing to play with
  Beside a mother-in-law.

I've been in the menagerie,
  All's to be seen I saw,
But the hyena took my fancy—
  Most like my mother-in-law!

I've thought about the devil,
  When conscious sin did gnaw,
But he at least had one peace—
  Never a mother-in-law.

MONEY.

Money is the mighty prince
  That rules o'er the nation,
It can grant your behest
  To ev'ry rank and station,

From an accoucheur's fee
  To religious consolation.

It's a balm for all your grief,
  It sweetens all your woes,
Puts the raiment on your back
  And stockings on your toes,
It's the talismanic sesame
  That opes society's doors.

'T will give you home, comfort, and ease
  Of life in every feature,
'T will help you to get a wife
  And then to impeach her;
With it you may bribe the devil,
  And the devil bribe the preacher.

It will likewise save your neck
  From the law's raging strife,
It can lead you safely through
  All of its passions rife;
Money is the winning card
  In ev'ry game of life.

Money is a sovereign grand,
  Whether in bonds or stocks,
For weal or woe 't is supreme
  In life's contending shocks,
And church and state are both alike,
  One great missionary-box.

You ragged saints boast a grace
  A wretched poverty's given,
And count it luck that wicked fate
  'Gainst all your plans has striven,
For money opens every gate
  Except the gate of heaven.

THE DYSPEPTIC.

His very soul was born in fear,
  A bloody God stood o'er him,
A flaming hell with tortures dire
  Yawned darkly before him;
His sun arose on fields of blood,
  His moon went down in woe,
Every cloud was a storm cloud
  With never a friendly bow.

When he essayed the religious,
  His torturing pains to beguile,
He saw blood from Calvary stream,
  But all mixed up with bile;
In those dark thoughts that diagnose
  A stomach ill at ease,
He saw his God in dusky frowns
  He never could appease.

With head downcast and face severe,
  In gloomy tones he speaks,
For every smile he sheds a tear
  To efface it from his cheeks;
He bows like one in funeral train,
  The last sad rites to honor,
Who follows closely on the bier,
  The only friend and mourner.

Now, when he's bilious and morose,
  'T is heavenly inspiring
To listen to his funeral groans
  About the dead and dying;
And what to me is stranger still,
  These frowns upon his face

Are worshiped by the common herd
  As evidence of grace.

Melancholia is superstitious,
  And *vice versa* they,
He who nurses an inward grief
  Must give it vent some way;
But why think we strange of deed
  With eccentric passion fraught,
The blood that courses thro' the brain
  Gives color to the thought.

IS IT NOT ENOUGH, MY BROTHERS?

Is it not enough, my brothers,
  We accept the terms of battle,
Are we indeed Freedom's peers,
  Or are we slavish cattle?
Is it not enough, my brothers,
  We quail before your blows,
Must we dismantle Southern graves
  To please our Northern foes?

We've felt the terrors of grim war,
  We shed our blood to satiate,
We came again and humbly begg'd
  A home within the State;
We're willing to forget the past,
  Willing to bury away its braves,
But ask us not, O my brothers,
  To desecrate their graves!

We dearly love America,
  We regret its civil shame,

And tho' we are the vanquished
    We bear not all the blame;
We can not crown with infamy
    The heroes of its cause,
Nor assign them to oblivion,
    Nor ask we for applause.

We struck, my friends, as we thought right,
    The shells flew hot and fast,
Nor till we could fight no more,
    Said we 't was our last;
But now extends the friendly hand
    'Cross the bloody chasm deep,
May flowers bloom on ev'ry field
    Where the rival heroes sleep.

And while the proudest Northern heart
    Rejoices o'er its loved braves,
Let children of the sunny South
    Reverence their fathers' graves;
Deck them with inglorious flowers
    And protect from ev'ry shame,
Be they martyrs or be they knaves,
    They 're our father's bones the same.

We bow before Fate's iron wheel,
    We shrink from war's alarms,
In our bosoms the spirit o' pride
    Appeals no more to arms;
O'er our fathers' moss-grown graves,
    O'er long dark years of waste,
We children offer hands and hearts
    In burial of the past.

THE UNDERTAKER.

Oh! I'm an undertaker
   Whom death has ne'er dismayed,
I love to bury my friend—
   And such is my trade;
Tho' with mourners in distress
   I sometimes force my tears,
'T is hard to weep, when trade's good,
   O'er other people's cares.

When all the people are healthy
   Doctors are very sad,
When nations are religious
   Missionaries are mad;
Who blames an undertaker
   For being in a flurry
When ev'ry body's fat and well
   And no one's to bury!

I know the hearse looks mournful
   With its long funeral train,
I know the wails of bereavement
   Fill all your hearts with pain;
Man had as well be cheerful
   And in heart forgiving—
There's profit in ev'ry woe
   Where some make a living.

I never but once felt sad
   With soul and heart's distress,
·It was when the tombstone man
   Condoled me on business;
For oh! he looked so haggard,
   He made me to repent

That I could n't bury myself
And buy a monument.

'T is undertake or starve, sir,
    Which would you prefer?
You can't expect me to weep
    With ev'ry customer;
I do n't wish my friends to die,
    My bosom warmer throbs,
But, if they *will* kick the bucket,
    Please give me the jobs.

FORTUNE.

Fortune is a fickle jade,
    A coquette of deceitful guile,
Howe'er much she favor you,
    Beware her inconstant smile.

To-day she smiles, to-morrow frowns,
    And laughs but to distress you,
Still practicing deceitful wiles
    Even tho' she caress you.

The dearest favors of her hand
    Are like the gaudy flower
That blossoms forth in radiant hues
    To wither in an hour.

Full oft' ye think her smiles secure,
    The fates in your behalf,
When murky clouds are gathering
    Darkly beyond your path.

Full oft her promised favors
    Are like a mirage fleet,

Leading on to a deeper wóe,
Mere specter of deceit.

Oh! know that fortune is fickle
With her smiles and her frowns,
And learn to take life easy then
In all its ups and downs.

KENTUCKY.

Old Kentucky's a saucy place,
Her people are a hardy race,
Ne'er rolled old Time thro' fairer scenes
Than gild her thousand winding streams;
In check or brass, wise men or fools,
We may succumb to foreign schools,
But in some things we are bosses,
At least in whiskies and horses—
Whiskies and horses are true to
Kentucky's boasted pride and beauty.
'T is not poets nor statesmen grand
Who spread our fame from land to land,
Nature's grandeur and beauty 's filled
With horses and copper-distilled;
Laugh who will at customs antique,
At dwellers on each mountain peak,
But even on the vintaged Rhine'
They lay aside the Bordeaux wine,
Scotch ale and gins all to the shade,
For whisky in Kentucky made.
So far as empires spread their sway
Or continents roll with the day,

Men use wines, opium, or hashish,
Kentucky Bourbon ne'er can perish;
Others boast literary pride,
Men of genius and culture wide,
Philosophers, poets, statesmen, and dandies—
Kentucky leads them all in flavored brandies.

ROYALTY.

Oh! what are kings,
    What kind of earth,
That to such things
    As royal birth,
True hearts and brave,
    On bended knee,
Must bow as slaves
    To majesty?

Does not one blood
    Through ev'ry heart
Pour its crimson flood
    From life's first start?
What lights, what sparks,
    That may decide
The lordly marks
    Of regal pride?

'T is history's page,
    In kindling fires,
Marks the lineage
    Of bloody sires;
'T is Freedom's wail
    By which we trace
The bloody trail
    Of lordly race.

'T is tyranny's blood
　And liberty's groans
Whence royal brood
　Secure their thrones;
Sad are the days,
　Degenerate the times,
Children are praised
　For their sires' crimes.

Are men but tools
　For ambition's good,
To feed proud fools
　For sake of blood?
Oh! cruel's the fate
　Allows such things,
Burdens the state
　For pride of kings.

My country pure,
　By heaven blessed,
No titled grandeur
　Upon thy breast:
Ev'ry man's descent
　Equal by birth,
A citizen president
　Elected for worth.

No lordly pleasures,
　Ignominious stains,
Deplete thy treasures
　For blood in its veins;
Born equal and free,
　Thy maxim e'er rings,
Life and liberty—
　Death to the kings!

EVOLUTION.

First of all, old Chaos ruled supreme
Where God before alone had been,
Broad and deep in nebulous waste,
Spread through the dusky realms of space;
Then condensed and liquefied to run
Into a central and molten sun,
Till by centrifugal power it hurls
To circling orbs, burning suns, and worlds.
Hissing and steaming in fiery wrath,
Earth flames a meteor 'long its path,
Till by radiation the heat expires
And a crust floats on internal fires;
Surging vapors in mad commotion
Condense into a boiling ocean,
The cooling ocean with it brings
Organic life in myriad things.
First to life, in point of time,
'Mid ocean's waste, was primitive slime
Washed from the sea-weeds and the rocks
By sportive waves in unconscious shocks;
A greasy scum was old primitive dad,
And his filthy lineage our sire monad,
Whence, by cellular segmentation,
Aggregation and proliferation,
Where cells on cells are multiplied,
Came man, creation's lord and pride.—
Proud man, with all his God-like boast,
Only condensed cellular chaos!
In centuries past, ere the tadpole
Was father of the human soul,
And this tadpole became a frog
And hopped about thro' gloomy bog,

Contemptuously eyeing the snail
That had neither vertebra or tail—
For science could ne'er on him bestow
The family pride of *genus homo*—
From low to high, by easy gradation,
Certain evolution marks creation :
Tadpoles, snakes, fish, then quadruped,
And so the proud lineage lead,
As light gleam'd o'er dusky chasm
Life enthused early protoplasm,
Light, the flame bursting on creation,
Life, the friction of cell proliferation,
The kangaroo became the donkey,
Then dropped his ears and was the monkey,
The monkey curtailed, his skull to expand,
Bloomed forth the perfect creature—man.

INHUMANITY.

Oh! what avails the Christianity
  Of this our Bible land,
Wherein so little humanity
  Thrives in the bosom of man.

Self, the all-ruling passion,
  Guides the baleful star of life,
And pride and avarice fashion
  All its seething strife.

Wails of woe, tears of distress,
  Still forever fill the earth,
The sorrows of the human breast
  Are as wide as mortal birth.

Who heeds the plaintive groanings
  Bubbling from the broken heart?

Who hears the dire mournings
  That disease and want impart?

Low on beds of affliction lie
  The sick with sad hearts bleeding,
A haughty world passes by,
  Their cries and wants unheeding.

By huts of poverty and wrong,
  Where famine broods hungry and gaunt,
Proud millionaires pass along
  As if misery had no want;

By dens of infamy and shame,
  Where beauty sleeps in foul embrace,
Self-righteousness pauses to blame,
  But ne'er with offers of peace.

Men seeking for gold and pleasure,
  No diff'rence how dear the gains,
Greedy avarice grasps the treasure
  Foul with dishonor's stains.

KISSES.

There is no joy to the heart so coy
  Like the thrill of a gentle kiss,
Only stolen pleasure can fill the measure
  With its exquisite bliss.

The gentle embrace, the smiling face,
  The eyes of love that greet you,
The rosy lips with nectar drips
  Leaning half way to meet you.

Oh, the thrill! it seems to fill
  The soul with blissful alloy,

To fondly press close to your breast
　The darling of your joy.

If aught of heaven to mortals given
　In that sweet moment's confessed,
So gently meek, with blushing cheek,
　Close she nestles to your breast.

She sighs, "oh, don't!" we think we won't,
　But, lest those eyes betray us,
They surely say indeed you may—
　Such looks never dismay us.

Some will pout their red lips out
　And threaten vengeance loud—
Don't be icy, just softly, nicely,
　There's sunshine behind the cloud.

E'en should they cry, who would deny,
　When Cupid's fancy rushes,
To kiss lightly 'way the tears that stray
　Among the rosy blushes.

There is no joy to the heart so coy,
　No moment so thoughtless of woe,
As when lips sweet each other meet
　With softest touch and slow.

CLOSE TO MY BREAST I CLASP MY DEAR.

Close to my breast I clasp my dear,
　Her arms around me twine,
She whispers softly in my ear,
　"Darling, I'm only thine."

From off her lips' vermilion hue,
  Where honeyed sweets repose,
I sip as bees would sip the dew
  From out the fragrant rose.

Gentle breezes fraught with perfume
  Sweep o'er beds of flowers,
And rarest birds are all in tune,
  So pass the pleasant hours.

First one fond clasp, then releasing,
  A blush, a kiss, and then
Another clasp, kisses unceasing,
  With blushes strown between.

The heaving breast, the gentle sigh,
  Eyes that languish calmly
As silver moons in summer's sky
  When night is soft and balmy.

Why talk to me of dreams of love?
  Oh! give me love that's real—
Only cold philosophy can move
  To love that's ideal—

Not visions ethereal and bright,
  Fairies fed on flowers,
Dancing where the silver moonlight
  Carpets fancy's bowers;

Not visions thin, like angel's wings,
  Nor shadowy like their faces,
But flesh and blood that fondly clings
  Responsive to embraces.

A throbbing heart, a glowing cheek,
  A warmth that may be felt,
Sweet laughing eyes and lips that speak,
  And what they think they tell 't.

ADIEU, MY LOVE, A LONG ADIEU.

Adieu, my Love, a long adieu!
   The wildest fancies of my heart
Ne'er dreamed that thou wast untrue,
   Yet cruel fate decrees we part;
Still, though the world is broad and wide,
   Where'er by chance I'm doomed to rove,
Thou'll be my constant thought, my pride,
   My song, my dream, and my love.

There are some souls to love benighted,
   And some have loved but loved in vain,
The sad love that has been slighted
   Wrings the heart with bitter pain;
But if there is anguish of heart,
   The bitterest mortals e'er endure,
'T is when love from love must part,
   Mutual, confiding, and true.

There's no woe to mortals given,
   In bereavement's torturing arts,
Like the grief that once has riven
   The tender chords of entwining hearts;
The human soul has no feeling,
   In sorrow's bitterest scope,
To keen sensibilities appealing,
   Than when bereft of love and hope.

There is a grief too deep for tears,
   Feelings that can find no vents,
Where woe smothers the soul with fears
   And bleeds the heart in silence;
Farewell, my Love, farewell forever,
   Till we meet never more to part!
Naught can stay the powers that sever
   Or heal the grief that wounds my heart.

THE INVALID.

Oh! here I lie and languish,
  While 'long each nerve and vein
Disease throbs in feverish anguish
  And darts with fiery pain ;
Sometimes I cry, when wond'ring why
  My strange fate is given,
Is it because of broken laws
  Or is 't the hand of Heaven ?

Poor, miserable, emaciated wretch,
  My time moves slowly away,
Torturing hours lengthen to months
  As drags the weary day ;
And as the night takes its flight
  I pray for the morrow,
The morrows come in sick'ning gloom,
  And all of life is sorrow.

Thus wearily from year to year
  Life drags its skeleton along,
As if I was but lingering here
  To brood o'er Nature's wrong,
Soothing my cares with briny tears,
  Cheering my drooping soul
By carving groans on tombstones
  While waiting for my goal.

I welcome death, and I brave
  The sickly fears of those who weep,
There is a peace within the grave,
  A sweet, long, and dreamless sleep ;
There in its peace each pain 'll cease
  And in oblivion rest.
My God, enfold my immortal soul
  Peacefully to Thy breast!

THE TRAGEDY.

She languished in an easy chair,
Slovenly dressed, disheveled her hair,
A graceful mien and queenly air,
 Sporting her swab and snuff;
Spit in the box, and rubbed her teeth
Till juice covered her chin beneath,
Stained her cheeks and fumed her breath,
 But still 't was not enough.

She propped her feet 'gainst the door,
Squirted ambier over the floor,
She fell asleep and then did snore,
 And dreamed the strangest dream;
She thought the world 'd come to an end
And she herself was to judge men,
There was no vice they could defend
 'Gainst condemnation keen.

First came whisky delirium tremens,
She hailed vicegerent of demons, .
Pronounced his doom with vehemence
 To dusky realms below;
But shook her sleep the demon base,
Glared wildly with a fiendish face,
Denied her right to judge his case
 With furious uproar.

High on her throne in state sublime
She mocked at his infernal crime,
The prince of woe in ev'ry clime
 Where there were souls to rob;
A frightful vision in her dream,
The demon throttled her 't would seem,
She woke in terror with a scream—
 She had swallow'd her swab.

ABSTRACTION.

To-night, as I sit thinking,
In my thoughts drinking
  The unfathomed depths of the sky,
Out through dreary waste,
Out through boundless space
  My unfettered fancies fly ;

Of worlds in circling flight,
Of time that's infinite,
  I think whence they all began ;
From this broad career,
Stoop to this little sphere
  To regard the state of man.

Some tiny unseen sprite,
From out the shades of night,
  Whispers to my abstracted mind,
How little art thou, man,
Insignificant thy plan
  Measured by Nature sublime ;

But an atom, a mite
In space that's infinite
  In weary waste of years forlorn,
Flickering spark of light
In an eternal night,
  A flash, and deep darkness rolls on.

But, lest our conscience belies, ·
A still small voice only cries,
  From all these thy soul'll sever ;
They indeed shall pass away
Till forgotten their day,
  Thou shalt live with God forever.

THE BLIND MAN.

Stranger, these shrunken, sightless orbs
  No radiant beauties trace,
But only rayless gloom absorbs
  The blackest realms of space;

The world in all its beauty sleeps,
  To me a sphere of gloom,
Not one ray its shadow sweeps
  E'en at the brightest noon.

Still, though I catch the mellow sound
  When 'wakes the world of light,
And day spreads its gladness around
  Where all to me is night,

Into these weeping eye-balls white
  No earthly vision's given,
I muse upon the glorious sight
  As I muse upon the heaven.

But in hope's sweet companion, faith,
  The darkest bosom's light
Is solace for a blacker death
  Than this—my life of night.

An inward consciousness has told
  That, beyond the azured skies,
A light shall dawn upon the soul
  Too bright for human eyes.

How sweet to think I yet may trace,
  'Mid swelling joys profound,
The contour of each friendly face
  Known only now by sound;

And when the central suns shall fade
In these dull eyes so blind,
Bright as when first they were made
The light of God shall shine.

——— —

NATURE IS LIKE THE STORMY OCEAN.

Nature is like the stormy ocean,
  Ever surging at its will,
Rolling in perpetual motion,
  A life that's never still.

Drifting on its current, sent
  Like cloud athwart the sky,
Mere creatures of the element,
  We rest only to die.

Life is like the raging storm,
  The roaring thunder's strife,
E'en the blood our bosoms warm
  Courses in streaming life.

Our restless hearts are beating
  In rhythm to each breath,
Nature's great lesson repeating,
  A calm is certain death.

From creation's stormy birth
  Unceasing motion's rife,
As the circling flight of earth,
  So moves the course of life.

So the thoughts of men are shifting
  On thought's restless ocean,
Like the wild currents drifting
  By winds in commotion.

Think not 't is a discordant chime
That bids Nature ne'er pause,
But a harmonious God sublime,
Immutable His laws.

Impious man, canst thou not find
Engraved on life's dark night
The movement of a hand divine,
Ruling in love and might?

BE KIND TO THE LIGHTNING-ROD MAN.

Be kind to the lightning-rod man,
Now, that he is dead,
Let them tread softly around
Who 've no tears to shed.

Perhaps, in the far-off West,
A fond sister or brother
Lift him on their prayers—
Perhaps 't is a mother.

Chilled in death's cold embrace
By Mercy's decree willed,
Wound up for a thousand years,
But now forever stilled.

Oh ! let not inquisitive man
Disturb his quiet sleep,
Bury him 'neath the willows
And plant him very deep ;

Place a rod upon his tomb
And epitaph his sand,
To warn the book agent
And patent medicine man.

GIVE ME DRINK, OH, GIVE ME DRINK!

Give me drink, oh, give me drink!
Why speak to me of souls who sink
  Into hell?
Why speak to me of sin and shame?
Through my veins there rolls a flame,
And fiery serpents hissing proclaim
  Its magic spell.

Give me drink, oh, give me drink!
I stand upon eternity's brink,
  My soul in sorrow,
For its magic spell has bound me,
Like a serpent coiled around me;
Give me drink and I will drown the
  Burning horror.

Give me drink, oh, give me drink!
Blear-eyed demons laughing, wink
  At my pains;
Though still living yet I'm cursed,
A slave to a frenzied thirst,
I scorn its power but can not burst
  Its chains.

Give me drink, oh, give me drink!
Sure 't is hell enough I think
  Manifest;
Why speak to me of burning fire?
My soul's bound by fierce desire,
My thirst kindles a demon's ire
  In my breast.

Give me drink, oh, give me drink!
Among its fumes let me sink,
Ne'er returning;
A slavish thirst, beastly pleasure—
Yet I'd squander heaven's treasure
And all eternity can measure
To soothe its burning.

WHY SHOULD WE GROW FAINT-HEARTED?

Why should we grow faint-hearted
Whene'er our sorrows come?
Is the light without its shadow,
The calm without its storm?
The darksome winter dreary,
With its somber hours,
Has chained in its icy arms
Spring-time's joyous flowers;

And e'en the gladsome sunshine
That cheers the harvest feast,
But for clouds that bring us rain
Would smile on desert waste.
You may not always see the light
Beam through the dusky clouds
When black despair hangs its drapery
Round you in mystic shrouds.

There's light beyond the darkness
The eye can not traverse,
It will shine round you brightly
When the clouds all disperse;

You may think the flowers dead
  And buried 'neath the snow,
They're waiting the spring-time
  To gather strength and grow;

You may think the night eternal
  While waiting for the dawn,
All its darkness will melt away
  Before the rosy morn;
You may think the hand unkind
  That fills your bed with thorns
When affliction weighs heavily
  Upon your tortured bones.

Cheer up, brothers, be not dismayed,
  Whate'er fate has given,
Howe'er the world may frown and hate
  Trust the smiles of heaven!
Think not that you are alone,
  Unanswered in your prayer,
When you kneel to God and Heaven,
  Sure there is mercy there.

LITTLE INNOCENT.

A little girl approached the coffin
  Where mother bow'd her head,
"Kiss me, papa, kiss me, papa,"
  Little Innocent said;
But ne'er a word from the coffin—
  Her papa was dead.

She followed the funeral train
  Quietly to the graveyard;

She saw a new grave yawning deep
  Within the grassy sward,
She saw the coffin lowered down
  And heard each falling clod;

She looked into her mother's eyes,
  She heard her plaintive groan,
Then gazed into the filling grave
  Where fast the sod was thrown;
And said she, with a swelling heart,
  "Papa's gone, papa's gone."

In their bereavement all alone,
  When the sad day had gone,
Little Innocent said to her ma,
  Seated by the hearth-stone:
"Bad men put papa in a hole,
  Let's go and bring him home."

THE CAMP MEETING.

The people herd in from afar
  Thro' the rain or sleetings,
The preachers too are gathering there
  To protract the meetings;
The saints have got their armors on,
  You may hear them shouting,
At ev'ry blast of gospel gun
  Old Satan is routing.

Some do shout and some do faint,
  Some teach the beginner,
While some heat up the icy saint,
  Some alarm the sinner;

Some clap their hands, some pull their hair,
  All like mad bulls roaring,
And some by preach and some by prayer
  Keep the spirit going,

Till soon the mourner's bench along
  Bow souls in sad contrition,
And while the priest beats on the gong
  The spirit works its mission;
Around the saints stand in array,
  Of saints there are no lack,
Some point the penitent the way,
  Some beat him on the back.

With howls and shouts and horrid din,
  Lest wicked spirits revel,
They frighten 'way the monster, sin,
  And vanquish the Devil;
They clap their hands, and round and round
  They march and sing and pray,
To coax the gentle spirit down
  While devils are at bay.

But stoop, ye angels from the skies,
  Hush, ye winds, your humming too,
See an athlete from the altar rise,
  See his soul is coming through!
Behold! he sweats, he foams, he growls,
  But wait, you'll see him prance,
He shakes himself and then he howls
  Till trees and fences dance.

And now the good work has begun,
  The Devil's in a flurry,
Incessant roars the gospel gun,
  They come through in a hurry;

As the flaming contagions spread
　Demons are laughed to scorn,
Every saint is hot till red
　And souls on souls are born.

Resonant woods and fields around
　With reverberation,
From hills and cliffs roll back in sound
　Wild echoes of damnation,
As shouts each saint or howls each fiend
　In search of new delusions,
Till all Bedlam seems pantomimed
　In raging confusions.

TO SOME YOUNG GIRLS ON THEIR RE- QUEST FOR A SONG.

You ask me for a song, sweet girls,
　Yet say not what to sing,
From pretty faces wreathed in curls
　The sweetest fancies spring;
If I should sing my heart would move
　At what your presence' bring,
I'd woo the muse that sings of love,
　Nor other song could sing.

Who has looked on pretty faces
　And yet controlled his will,
Who beheld such charming graces
　And never felt their thrill?
No poet he in Nature's thoughts,
　For true beauties inspire,

Wild discord screaks in broken notes
  From off his rusty lyre.

Nature has in this serred world
  Many a vision bright,
But nothing like a fair, sweet girl,
  Whose soul and heart are right;
How innocent and artless she,
  Unstained by selfish guiles,
From cunning and deception free,
  Are all her pleasant smiles.

When life's bitter cup's filled with grief,
  There's comfort in her tears,
When filled with joy, however brief,
  She smiles upon our cares;
She has a sigh for all our fears,
  A smile for ev'ry bliss,
What woes she may not drown in tears,
  She smothers with her kiss.

Oh then, sweet girls, know well the part
  Nature's bounty's given,
The treasures of a pure heart
  Bear exchange in heaven;
Remember that the fairest face
  Will wither and decay,
The immortal mind by God's grace
  Alone may live for aye.

There is a beauty hid within,
  A beauty of the heart,
That will outshine the fairest skin
  Polished by human art;
For that beauty, my dear sweet girls,
  I'd have you strive and win,

A treasure worth a thousand worlds
All wrapt in woe and sin.

And now, sweet girls, I need not sing
How much I wish you well,
May roses 'long your pathway spring,
Fairer than I can tell;
And ere touched by time's magic wand
Withers ev'ry flower,
May all your days and years expand
In pleasure's sweetest bower.

TO MISS MARY AND HER HORSE.

We were called some miles in the country to dress a fractured limb. Miss Mary sent her riding horse for us to drive in our buggy. When we arrived at the patient's house, Miss Mary very unceremoniously demanded her horse. We hired a mule, and got home as best we could.

Our dear Miss Mary,
Quite contrary,
   Left us in the cool,
But a doctor
Brooks no proctor,
   He can drive a mule.

Called by duty,
Defied by beauty,
   We felt just like a fool,
And in the mud,
Till another flood,
   Had stuck but for the mule.

Formed so neatly,
Divinely, sweetly,
   We bowed before her graces,

Only a horse
Could mend our loss
   More than pretty faces.

But we were spunky,
We drove the donkey
   To the tune of many raps,
For we were as gay
As birds in May,
   You guess the reason perhaps.

Cold is the heart
That can impart
   Naught but its dreary gloom,
That has no smile
That may beguile
   The stranger, worn, from home.

Now, dear Miss Mary,
Even a fairy
   May sometimes act amiss,
But we forgive thee,
Long, long live thee,
   Thine pe peace, content, and bliss.

If some other day
We come thy way
   We'll be our own bosses,
God bless thy soul!
Bet all thy gold,
   We'll drive our own horses.

THE JUDGMENT DAY.

The judgment day has come at last,
Time's relegated to the past,
Over earth's dark and howling waste
    Damnation broods on pinions black;

Deep darkness hovers like a shroud
Vailing the earth in mystic cloud,
And groaning thunders trumpet loud
    The coming of our Lord and King.

The quivering rocks are breaking,
The mountains to and fro shaking,
The earth trembling, rocking, quaking,
    Throughout all nature is convulsed.

Hark! the Lord of glory is come,
He rides upon the thunder-storm,
A vial of wrath He pours among
    All of the living sons of men.

The bursting graves their dead outpour,
The surging waves dash them ashore,
Death and hell are forced to restore
    The bodies and the shrieking souls.

The earth melts with a fervent heat,
The heaven rolls a fiery sheet,
One glance of God, ruin's complete,
    And all Nature's laws are chaos.

But first before the judgment throne,
With shouts of joy or bitter groan,
From death, from hell, from heaven torn,
    The sons of Nature are arrayed;

The wicked flee in sore despair,
Calling on rocks and mountains bare
To hide them from the lightning glare
    Of God Almighty's searching eye;

The righteous with victorious song
The sulphurous caves of hell prolong,
Heaven echoes in thunders strong,
    "Our Lord, the God of glory reigns."

The judgment's o'er, chaos supreme,
Eternal night with dusky sheen
Vails the scenes where time has been,
    But time is no more forever.

THE TOOTHACHE.

Why this infernal pang invented,
Unless to try the soul demented?
He who the live-long night can take,
A martyr to its torturing ache,
Nor curse, nor pray, nor make complaint,
May well be canonized a saint.

OLD AGE STEALS ON APACE.

Old age steals on apace,
    Like shadows o'er the dial,
Wrinkles creep 'long the face,
    Smothering ev'ry smile;
Glad hours of merry youth
    Are shadowed by decay,

27

Scarcely we feel its truth
　Before we pass away;
Gray-haired men seared with age,
　'Long time's ruthless windings,
Stand pictured on each page
　For solemn remindings;

We gaze on their white locks,
　And mark their shrunken forms,
As on the riven rocks
　Weathered by ancient storms.
They say with kindest smile:
" Our days are few and cold ;
Yesterday but a child,
　To-day we 're growing old,
The morrow 'll blow its blast
　Above our quiet graves,
Time's magic touch will waste
　Itself on other slaves.

" Ye who in rosy youth
　Are chasing fleeting joys,
Time 's pitiless and ruth
　Despite your phantom toys,
Life 's a delusive dream,
　An *ignis fatuus* bright,
Ye chase the changing gleam　　•
　'Mid doubts dark as the night."
Be our hope and faith bright,
　And when our sun may set
We 'll look through its twilight
　With no thoughts of regret.

I LOVE YOU.

I love you, I love you, my own sweet girl,
　With a passion that's stronger than death,
I would not desert you for all the world,
　The world'd be void of you bereft;
You are my dream, my joy, my very life,
　Inspiration of my being,
The hope that illumes the world's darkest strife,
　Before which all cares are fleeing.

EPITAPH ON A PRIEST.

Here lies a priest, peace to his soul,
　His life he misused it,
We will not say, now that he's cold,
　That he e'er abused it.
As 't is good for society
To keep a great variety,
So the priest and Devil betwixt
The ins and outs of life commixed;
Weep not o'er his moldering form
Wasted by the dissolving storm.
We will all get together
　In the great great coming feast;
The priest leads the people
　And the Devil leads the priest.

TO M—.

My sweet, my pretty,
My darling M—,
　　I will live for thee;
By this token
My vow's spoken,
Ne'er to be broken
　　Till all eternity.

Yes, 't is heaven
That has given
　　Bright rays from above;
Thy smiles shining,
My soul inclining,
My heart entwining
　　With tenderest love.

By life's pleasure
The greatest treasure
　　Love can e'er impart;
I adore thee,
I implore thee
To restore me
　　In thy loving heart.

A passion blind,
A fate unkind
　　May drive hope away,
Still in my soul
Thou shalt hold
Supreme control
　　Fore'er and for aye.

HOW DOCTORS MAY MAKE MONEY.

In answer to the inquiry in the Louisville Medical News,
"How Shall the Doctors make more Money?"

To all the impecunious doctors,
The pill and potion concoctors,
Who'd learn the secrets of money,
To buy clothes or bread or honey :
Money's the root of all evil,
Companion of saint and devil,
Laws sacerdotal and civil,
It brings all men to a level ;
'T will buy the soul, 't will buy the brain,
'T will nerve the heart and soothe its pain,
To ev'ry rank it will instate—
Money is king beyond debate.
Ye noble sons of Esculapius
Why whet your rusty rapiers ?
Out of the ruts, out the bushes,
Time moves as a mad stream rushes
When 't would break its tortuous bed
And flow where wilder waters lead ;
Think ye the medical profession
From other trade's a digression ?
Are ye saints on righteousness fed,
Or lab'rers for your daily bread ?
Are ye philanthropists instead,
Poor toilers at an honest trade,
Or are ye conceited asses,
Moving round with saintly faces,
Drumming for a social station
'Bove poor doctors' elevation ?
Humble your pride, be not conceited
By pill and puke your rank's meted ;

What's the lot of pill refiners
More'n the lot of sausage-grinders?
Only trichinous sausage kills
As surely as the doctor's pills;
Should he who kills be nobler bred
Than he who but inters the dead,
Or do ye think your bitter draught
Gives out sweet thoughts when it is quaffed?
Suppose your calomel and quinine
Should hear the deaf or sight the blind,
The ear-trumpeter has such fame,
The spectacle-man does the same;
Or should he have the louder cheers
Who washes wax out of our ears?
Shall we give only him the prize
Who burns the warts off of our eyes?

Why talk about "ethical code"
Honor to rule your jealous brood?
Hippocrates, in all his dote,
Invented this sham of a coat,
A glittering gloss to gull the fools—
The great would make the weak their tools.
Do n't boast too much of your science,
More in theory than appliance,
Nor boast too high its modern mission
Wrapped in ancient superstition;
The nine fried mice for epilepsy,
Rooster testes for dyspepsia,
Album grecum and urine spirits,
Equal some of modern merits;
As to dung by eagles muted,
Ne'er calomel more reputed,
Then the spells, the charms, and sage looks
Were worth a hundred modern books.

The question is, if there's any,
" How poor doctors may make money."
Behold the toiler with his spade,
Doubtless he earns what he has made;
Behold the cobbler driving pegs,
And so he lives, unless he begs;
See the smith, strong as a lion,
Beats his wealth from steel and iron;
Hear the priest in fervent desire,
Makes his living howling hell fire;
See the lawyer frauds concealing,
Help other rogues by his stealing;
To such like ways you may appeal,
To honest work or legal steal.
The priest's a mule of feeble bray,
There's little made by preach or pray;
As to the smith and his proctors,
They're most too honest for doctors.
True, there is fraud in ev'ry field,
But from bad pills there's no appeal;
The world, 't is true, has cash to waste,
But not on the mere pride of caste.
Who'd live by what he is knowing
Must keep his horn fore'er blowing;
Heed not professional disputing,
For patients not ethics tooting,
Then throw your code where the pig swills
And make your living selling pills.
To younger doctors this I say,
Advertise in a business way,
So many a man wins cash respects
Who'd starve upon jealous ethics;
Sure ye're not a lot of donkeys
To be rode by menagerie monkeys,

To sit and starve licking your paws
O'er some old Hippocratic laws.
This world is like a busy hive,
The drones must die, toilers survive,
.But royal rogues to honor born—
Ev'ry chicken must scratch his own corn.

SENTIMENTS OF THE YOUNG MISS.

Will not some beau his time forego,
   By his presence cheer me,
I live alone at my father's home,
   Never a beau comes near me.

I'm sweet sixteen, close in between
   My maiden and womanhood,
I curl my tresses, I wear long dresses,
   And really I think I should.

I've a pretty face, a delicate waist,
   A heart in which no care is;
And then my feet are trim and neat,
   My lips are just like cherries.

With those I meet out on the street
   I have never learned to flirt,
I've had no flame that's worth the name,
   My heart is whole and unhurt.

Although I'm shy, I'd not deny
   My smiles if you'd be basking;
Just of the age the female sage
   Gives her heart for the asking.

No studied art to ensnare the heart
   With cold passions distressing,

You name the day, I'll come half way,
  And we'll ask papa's blessing.

A lock of hair, a kiss as rare,
  I freely will bestow them;
An elderly miss would frown at this
  Awful breach of decorum.

When I am older and my heart colder,
  Perhaps I too will refuse,
Like elder maidens with ethics laden,
  And stand on my P's and Q's.

A NEGRO'S SERMON ON A THEOLOGY WITHOUT A HELL, AND THE NEW VERSION OF THE TESTAMENT.

Come boss, I's hearn dat de gospel
  Am chang'd much its station,
What den'll follow, who can tell,
  De next improved translation;
Old hell am tumbled to hades,
  De fires am all gone out,
De birds singin' in de shade-trees
  Whar de 'ternal waters spout.

Some 'tend de debel howls no more,
  Dat he am all a miff,
White folks hab improvised his roar
  To skeer poor niggers wiff;
Folks, if you stop the debel's snort
  De church hab no correction,
De mission money will be short,
  Hen-roosts widout protection.

28

White priests may a livin' pursue
  Drummin' politic cabal,
What 'll de poor nigger preachers do
  Widout their hell and debel?
Dese fifty years I's sarved de Lord
  Nor compromised wid fashions,
Still I propose to preach de word
  Dat brings de most rations.

Why talk about de golden harp
  An' leab out de Old Scratch?
De nigger 'rise and wiff a yarp
  Go straight for your mellyun patch;
Why talk about de radiant skies
  Widout an impious snake?
If you 'd fotch tears in nigger's eyes
  Talk 'bout de fiery lake.

I 'll get me a keg of brimstone,
  Preach 'bout holy 'lection,
And when dem niggers howl and groan
  I 'll take up de collection;
I 'll paint de debel wiff big horns,
  A hell dat am not funny,
Take possum hide, ingans, or corn,
  When dey 're short ob money.

Now all you priests who preach like goats,
  Widout a hell for sinners,
You 'll get no more black cloth coats
  Nor chickens for your dinners,
De empty mission box repeating
  Your empty stomach's features;
Give me a hell hot, still heating,
  To fatten up de preachers.

THE GRAVE OF THE INDIAN CHIEF, IN THE INDIAN GRAVEYARD ON GREEN RIVER, KENTUCKY.

'T is only a mound, a grassy mound,
  Hid deep in the wilds away,
A few rude flints are scattered round—
  Relics of another day—

Near the clifts where Green River flows,
  But above its highest tide,
Where the tall oak heavenward grows
  And spreads far its branches wide;

Here, in a quiet mound, there sleeps
  A prince, the chief of his tribe,
Where only the midnight wind weeps
  In cadence with the dark tide.

In years far passed and gone for aye,
  · Ere white man had trod the ground,
He led his braves in fierce array
  O'er the hills and valleys round.

In these streams he netted for fish,
  And on these hills chased the deer,
And 't was his hope, his fondest wish,
  To have his bones buried here;

For here his father's manes repose,
  And here rest many true braves,
Whom legends dark will ne'er disclose,
  Brooding fore'er 'bove their graves.

So when his soul had ta'en its flight
  To dark realms of the never,

They buried him too in this lone site—
   Here let him rest forever.

But round each cliff and stream and hill
   Gather their shadowy forms,
Where sounded once their war-songs shrill
   Or calumet curled its fumes.

But let them rest here in each mound,
   Disturb not their quiet graves,
They sleep where death stills all renown
   Of mighty chieftain and braves.

No more the echoing wilds round
   Resound to their martial tread,
They rest within their ancient ground,
   Numbered with the millions dead.

Now none may tell their tales of strife,
   Their sad hopes or loves or feuds,
Nor wake again the scenes of life
   That once broke this solitude.

NIHILISM.

Hark! the dynamite bomb
   From its secret cave!
'T is the cry of oppression,
   The wail of the slave.

Let the tyrants tremble
   In proud opulence,
The king has his power,
   The slave his defense.

'T is music, 't is music!
  In thunders let 't ring,
The people's replying
  To rights of the king.

All the powers of heaven,
  Nor terrors of hell
Bristling with bayonets,
  Can cool the hot shell.

Though the kings are divine
  In blood and in bones,
The millions are enslaved
  To prop up their thrones.

Call 't a fiend if you will,
  The dynamite bomb.
'T is Liberty's groanings
  From its darkest tomb.

Slaves may languish in chains
  Or starve in dark cells,
But Oppression's last wail
  Is a wail of shells.

www.ingramcontent.com/pod-product-compliance
Lightning Source LLC
Chambersburg PA
CBHW060517030726

47498CB00004B/980